A Case of
BLACKMAIL IN BELGRAVIA

A Freddy Pilkington-Soames Adventure Book 1

CLARA BENSON

MOUNT
STREET
PRESS

Copyright

clarabenson.com

Cover, interior design and typesetting by Colleen Sheehan
wdrbookdesign.com

Cover spine and back by Shayne Rutherford
WickedGoodBookCovers.com

AUTHOR'S NOTE

I WOULD LIKE to extend my apologies to the present occupants of number 25, Caroline Terrace, London, for depositing a dead body outside their front door.

CHAPTER ONE

IT WAS A splendid dinner at Babcock's. The restaurant was crowded and noisy, and the atmosphere festive. The manager had given them the best table, knowing that to do so was to ensure that the name of the establishment would, sooner or later, be cited in the society pages as having been the setting for yet another gathering of some of London's most fashionable and influential personages, since it was an open secret that at least one member of the party wrote a gossip column for one of the popular papers. Forty years after its founding, Babcock's, with its gilded ceilings, grandly arched alcoves and marble columns imported especially from Italy, was by now a venerable stalwart of Piccadilly, and relied heavily on its reputation as the 'old dependable' among the higher classes. Other restaurants came and went, their stars burning brightly but briefly, but still Babcock's went on, a superior and a safe pair of hands, with every intention of continuing for another forty years or more. Respectable as it was, it had not the slightest objection to being mentioned in the occasional breathless report as the place in which such-and-such a person had found his wife dining in guilty company with the husband of another, and a scene had been narrowly avoided; or in which two senior Members of the Opposition had hatched a plot to overthrow their leader; or in which one society beauty had snubbed another cruelly and publicly. That was merely good business, and Babcock's was perfectly happy to be known as a place where one might dine superbly and perhaps catch a whiff of scandal at the same time—although, naturally, it affected to be entirely unaware of the less salubrious facets of its existence, as enumerated with feigned disapproval in some of the lower publications.

This evening, the crowd was a mixed one. It was a Thursday night, one of the busiest nights for Babcock's, since on Friday many of the usual clientèle would be going down to the country for the weekend, so many of the regulars were there, along with a number of foreigners, politicians, theatre-goers, business-men and even one or two film people. They had mostly been placed at tables towards the side of the room, where they might discuss confidential business or conduct illicit liaisons with a degree of privacy if so inclined. Not so the party in question, however, who were for the most part a raucous group and wholly accustomed to being looked at; indeed, would have been most offended to be ignored—the ladies in particular. They had been placed at a table in the very centre of the room, happy to act as unpaid entertainment for everybody else, secure in the knowledge that they were quite the most interesting and important people there. Many of the out-of-towners were already darting furtive glances at them, wondering who they might be.

The first to catch the attention—as always—was the golden-headed Mrs. Blanche Van Leeuwen, dressed all in white (an affectation of hers, as befitted her name). Now forty-two and on her second marriage, her days as a 'toast' long behind her, she was nevertheless still a beauty, able to turn heads wherever she went, although these days casual observers were less likely to remember who she was, or recall the triumph of her first season in England following her arrival from Australia. More immediately recognizable was the man to her left: Captain Maurice Atherton, the celebrated explorer. After his last expedition, in which he had nearly lost his life in the jungles of South America, he had announced that he was retiring to write his memoirs, although many said the spirit of adventure had not left him, and that he would not suffer to live a quiet life in England for long. From Captain Atherton, the gaze passed to the fashionably thin Nancy Beasley and then immediately darted about in search of her husband, who was sitting across the table from her. The marriage of Denis and Nancy Beasley was followed with great interest by the general public, since it was considered something of a miracle that they were still married at all, given Denis Beasley's penchant for the company of young ladies of the chorus, and Nancy's loud and public rage whenever she caught him at it. Theirs had been a volatile relationship from the start, and most of it, seemingly, had been conducted under the public eye, much to the disgust of Nancy's father, the late munitions millionaire. After ten stormy years of marriage never blessed by children, those in the know said it was only a matter of time before their names appeared in the divorce courts. On Nancy's left was Lady Bendish, widow of Sir Henry Bendish, the inventor and philanthropist. Willowy, drooping, and with a mournful, almost tragic air about her, she was listening politely to Denis, who seemed to be telling her an amusing anecdote. To the left of Denis was a small, bird-like woman with bright eyes that darted about constantly. Cynthia Pilkington-Soames was perhaps the least recognizable of the party, but also the most dangerous, since she it was whose column appeared each week in the *Clarion*, so it was always best not to get on her wrong side, lest one find oneself unflatteringly portrayed in that week's paper—or worse, not mentioned at all. Under the nom-de-plume of 'Robin,' she wrote of gay evening-parties, described the latest outrageous frocks sported by well-known beauties, dropped hints of scandals and *affaires*, and, with one stroke of her pen, could make or ruin a reputation for a whole season. Every Friday friends and foes alike scoured the page eagerly, to see whether Cynthia had anything to say about them, and felt alternately relieved or slighted depending on the result. That evening, indeed, there had been some little tension between Cynthia and Mrs. Van Leeuwen, who was smarting at the unfounded suggestion, in last week's column, that she had been lying about her age, and was in fact nearer fifty than forty. Barbed remarks sugar-coated with tinkling laughter had passed back and forth between the two ladies all evening, and it had taken all the diplomatic finesse of the man who sat between them to prevent mutual tensions from descending into open warfare.

It was odd that, though the table was a round one, nobody could have doubted that this last gentleman mentioned sat at the head of it, and was the most important member of the party. Nicholas Maltravers, or 'Ticky,' as he was known to his many close friends, was a man whom any reader of the society pages would recognize immediately, since not a ball, or a party, or a picnic, or a wedding was held without his being invited. When society matrons drew up their guest lists, they would invariably add, 'Oh, and Ticky, of course.' If there was an empty chair to be filled at a private dinner, Ticky was the man who would be called upon to fill it. Every page of his diary had something in it—so much so that he might have chosen never to dine at home if he liked. He was invited to everything, and could afford to pick and choose. He was a bon-vivant perched at the very pinnacle of society, although nobody could quite say how he had achieved this position, since he did not seem to be celebrated for anything in particular. He was certainly not known for his looks, being past fifty and of unhealthily sleek and glistening appearance, with hooded eyes and a curved smile that might almost have been described as a knowing smirk. His general habits and dealings with others did not bespeak any particular virtue of character. His wit could best be described as laboured. Nor did he throw parties of his own, but contented himself with attending those of his acquain-tances, at which he was sure to be surrounded by a crowd of well-wishers, who shrieked delightedly at his pithy observa-tions and seemed to want nothing more than to be admitted to his inner circle of friends. How he had attained his exalted status was a mystery, therefore, and it could only be supposed that he had managed it by a sort of osmosis, or perhaps even a magical charm. Whatever the case, and whether fair means or foul had been employed, he certainly seemed to relish the attention, and even accept it as his due.

That evening was no different. He was fêted and loved by his guests, his every comment agreed with, his every witticism seized upon and laughed uproariously at. If the party was the centre of attention at Babcock's, he was the centre of attention of the party. He dined lavishly, because it was his birthday, and because although the restaurant was an expensive one, nobody would have dreamt of letting him pay. The other gentlemen ate heartily, while the women ate little, or affected to. The caviare and oysters were declared to be the freshest anyone had ever tasted, and were washed down with a most invigorating Chablis, while the turtle soup was neither too hot nor too cold, and went beautifully with the sherry. The salmon and new potatoes were cooked to perfection, and were accompanied by a bottle of Montrachet from one of the oldest vineyards in France. After the roast venison, which all agreed was as tender as spring lamb, and which was served with an intriguing red Claret, there followed ices and petits-fours, complemented by a fine Muscat. Nobody had room for a savoury, and so the order for coffee was issued, and the ladies glanced significantly at one another and then at Ticky.

'Ticky, darling,' said Nancy Beasley, bringing out something from under the table. 'It's time for your present.'

Ticky assumed a look of combined surprise and modesty as the little gift-wrapped box was presented amid rowdy applause and squeals of excitement.

'I believe you are spoiling me,' he said. He smiled around at them all, and then carefully unwrapped the gift and brought out a little silver flask, of the sort that fits in a pocket.

'Look, it's engraved,' said Cynthia.

'So it is,' said Ticky. 'How perfectly delightful.'

'May I see?' said Blanche Van Leeuwen. She took the flask and exclaimed over it, then passed it to Captain Atherton, who also wanted to look at it. The little silver flask was passed from hand to hand around the table, since although all had contributed, not all had seen it. Ticky took it again and regarded it with polite interest.

'But you must try it, Ticky,' said Nancy. 'Don't let it be one of those presents that's never used.'

The knowing smile played around Ticky's mouth again, and he glanced up slyly at the other two men.

'I believe I shall,' he said. He summoned the waiter. 'Do you still have any of the 1820 Cusenier?' he said.

The waiter replied in the affirmative.

'Then you'd better bring it,' said Ticky. 'We'll have the whole bottle.'

The smiles on the faces of the other two men became wooden at the thought first of the cost, and second of such a flagrant waste of good Cognac. The bottle was brought and a large measure decanted into the flask. Ticky looked around.

'How splendid to have such true friends,' he said, with every appearance of sincerity. 'A toast. To you, my dears.'

He raised the flask and took a large mouthful, then another.

'Delicious,' he said, as the other men eyed the remainder of the Cognac still in the bottle.

'Here, take this and share it with the kitchen staff,' said Ticky to the maître d'hotel, who was hovering nearby.

The man was fulsome in his thanks, and the expressions of Denis Beasley and Captain Atherton became more wooden still as the bottle was carried off and placed carefully to one side.

The dinner was paid for, and there was a great fussing and stirring as everybody stood up, while at the other tables conversations were paused briefly as all the other diners took the opportunity to stare at the party as they left. Then they all moved out into the chilly October night, walking unsteadily (for a great deal of wine had been consumed) and calling out extravagant praises to the maître d'hotel as they went. And then they were gone, and everybody went back to what they had been doing, while the waiters raised their eyebrows at one another.

Outside, there was some little bustle as the arrangements for returning home were decided. Mrs. Van Leeuwen summoned her motor-car, in which there was room to carry three other people at a pinch, and offered to take the Beasleys and Lady Bendish home, pointedly ignoring Cynthia Pilkington-Soames. Captain Atherton lived nearby on Dover Street and intended to walk home, since he was in need of some air, he said. He cut short their goodbyes and went off with a wave. There was much kissing and exclaiming among the women, and much promising to telephone the next day, then Mrs. Van Leeuwen's car departed in great state, and somehow Cynthia found herself in a taxi to Belgravia with Ticky Maltravers, who lived in Caroline Terrace.

'Well, that was a most delightful evening,' said Cynthia. 'It's such a pity Herbert had to entertain that dull man from the bank at the last minute and couldn't come. Thank you, Ticky.'

'It was my pleasure,' said Ticky, graciously, as though he had paid for it. He was looking rather pink and uncomfortable. 'I fear I may have over-eaten, however,' he said.

'Oh, goodness,' said Cynthia. 'Perhaps a little digestive when you get home will do the trick.'

'I dare say it will,' he replied.

They sat in silence as the cab rounded Hyde Park Corner. Cynthia noticed that Ticky was breathing heavily and that he had begun to perspire freely.

'Dear me, you don't look well at all,' she said. 'What about a nip of brandy now? You have the little flask we gave you.'

'Perhaps you are right,' he said.

He brought out the flask from his pocket and fumbled with the cap, then took a mouthful of the Cognac and coughed.

The taxi drew up.

'Eaton Terrace,' the driver announced.

Cynthia alighted, as did Ticky, with difficulty.

'I think I shall walk the rest of the way,' he said. 'I dare say the fresh air will do me good.'

The taxi departed and Cynthia hurried up the steps to her smart front door and looked for her key. Ticky was standing on the pavement, swaying gently, and she glanced at him in concern.

'Are you sure you're all right, Ticky?' she said.

He opened his mouth to say something, and then took a step forward, as though he wanted to come into the house with her.

'I—' began Cynthia, and then uttered a little shriek of disgust as Ticky fell heavily against the railings and proceeded to be sick on the steps.

'Well, really!' she exclaimed, retreating. 'I should have thought you might have held it in until you got home.'

But Ticky Maltravers was beyond listening to anything. He slid down the railings to a sitting position, and remained there, fighting for breath and twitching slightly. It had at last occurred to Cynthia that something was very wrong.

'Ticky!' she said.

He lifted his head and fixed her with a hollow stare.

'Poisoned!' he said in a hoarse whisper, and with that, expired.

Cynthia stood for a second in astonishment, then looked about her as though she suspected someone of playing a taste-less joke on her. She moved gingerly forward, being careful not to tread in the remains of Ticky's last birthday dinner, and touched his cheek. There was no response. Carefully she lifted an eyelid. One eye stared balefully back at her. There was no doubt at all that he was dead.

'Oh, dear me,' said Cynthia.

CHAPTER TWO

ELSEWHERE, FREDDY Pilkington-Soames had had a most pleasant evening, having passed it in indulging in youthful high spirits at a fashionable new night-club near Regent Street. At two o'clock he and his friends reluctantly obeyed the order to vacate the premises, and emerged into the London night, preparing to head homewards and sleep the sleep of the just. Freddy was feeling quite delightfully fuzzy in the head, having that evening discovered a new type of cocktail containing champagne, Cointreau, Bourbon whisky, and a secret ingredient which he could not identify, but which was half-sweet and half-sour and rounded the whole thing off deliciously. The more he drank of it, the better it tasted, and since Freddy was a keen and scientific seeker of pleasure—indeed, could wax quite philosophical on the subject at times—he had judged it only right to experiment exhaustively in order to ascertain to his own satisfaction that no greater joy was to be had on that particular evening, at least. The result was that by the time he left the night-club, his brain and his finer motor abilities had mutually agreed to part company for a few hours. No matter, however; the world was a beautiful place, and Freddy felt not the misery of life's travails as he tottered gently towards Oxford Street in search of a taxi, a beatific smile on his face. Had any malefactor chosen at that moment to jump out in front of him with a dagger or a pistol and demand monies, it is very likely that Freddy would have pressed his last shilling upon the man, given him his hat for good measure, and sent him on his way with a cheery wave, so well-disposed was he towards the world in general.

After an abortive attempt to flag down a private motor-car, Freddy eventually managed to procure himself a taxi. He was just about to pronounce his destination to the driver, when he was rudely shoved aside.

'Pont Street,' said a familiar voice. 'Come on, Freddy, get in. You're holding the man up.'

It was his friend Mungo Pruitt, who had leapt into the conveyance before him, and who now reached out and pulled him in. The driver set off. Freddy's mind was not working as fast as it ought, and it took him a good few moments to realize that Pont Street was in the opposite direction from the one he wanted, for Freddy worked an honest living as a pressman of sorts, and had recently taken rooms near the offices of his newspaper, so as to be saved the inconvenience of having to spend more than five minutes in travelling to work of a morning.

'But I don't want to go to Pont Street,' he said, moving his mouth carefully, since his faculty of speech was not at its best at present. 'Pont Street is in quite the wrong place.'

'What are you talking about?' said Mungo. 'It's where I live.'

'But I want to go to Fleet Street,' said Freddy.

'Fleet Street be damned,' said Mungo. 'Why would anybody want to go to Fleet Street at this time of night? Or at any time, in fact? It's full of oily little men with pencils and cameras, whose only object in life is to catch one in the act of doing something unspeakable.'

This was a point with which Freddy could not truthfully disagree, and yet the fact remained that he did not wish to go to Pont Street. By the time he had succeeded in formulating in his head an unanswerable argument for getting his own way, however, the taxi had already arrived at Pont Street and Mungo had leapt out.

'Listen,' said Freddy, who was now ready to present his case. He jumped out after Mungo, preparing to give a long and impassioned speech as to the desirability of having instructed the driver to go East first, rather than West, but before he could begin, Mungo had paid the driver and the taxi had pulled away without him.

'Hi! Dash it,' said Freddy, waving desperately at the departing vehicle. 'Mungo, you ass, what the devil did you do that for?'

'Do what?' said Mungo. 'We're home, aren't we?'

'You might be,' said Freddy. 'But I'm not. I want to go to Fleet Street.'

'Oh, do you? I thought you were joking,' said Mungo. 'Still, I'm sure there must be a taxi around here somewhere. And now it's off to bed for me. Don't stand there too long, old chap. It's cold out here. Cheerio!'

And with that, he was off, leaving Freddy standing in a deserted street, a good three miles from home. Lesser men might have railed against a similar inconvenience; not Freddy. The night was cold and all he wanted at present was to find a comfortable bed—any bed might do—and collapse into it for eight hours or so. If Fleet Street were denied him, then let another sanctuary receive him. A short distance away was the house his mother used when she was in London, for which he had a key. She would most likely be tiresome about his current condition, but it was late, and perhaps he could creep in without being heard.

He set off unsteadily down Chesham Street, and within a very few minutes was turning into Eaton Terrace. The house was dark; perhaps nobody was at home—which possibility suited Freddy very well, since he was more afraid of his mother's sharp tongue than he cared to admit. He felt in his pocket for a key and, after a few false tries, succeeded in inserting it into the lock. It turned, and the door gave way more suddenly than he had expected. It immediately hit an obstacle—something soft yet unyielding—and at the same time he heard a shriek. He pushed at the door and felt someone push back from the other side.

'Go away!' a voice said frantically. Freddy recognized it as that of his mother.

'What are you doing?' said Freddy. 'Let me in.'

'Freddy!' exclaimed Cynthia. 'You frightened me half to death! Quick, come in!'

The door opened a little way and he was able to squeeze in. The entrance-hall was almost dark, with only a little light coming in through the glass above the door.

'Why are you standing here in the dark?' said Freddy. 'And who's this on the floor?' For he could feel with his foot that the obstacle blocking the front door was human.

'Shh! Not so loud!' hissed Cynthia. 'It's Ticky.'

'Ticky?'

Freddy's brain was by no means operating at full capacity, but he felt it might matter less if he could see. He groped along the wall and switched on the light. Cynthia gave a little squeak. Freddy regarded his mother, who was shrinking against the wall, wide-eyed, still in her evening-dress and fur coat, and then turned his attention to the thing on the floor. Ticky was lying still and supine on the black and white tiles, eyes closed. His face was white.

'You're right, it is Ticky,' said Freddy. 'Why's he sleeping there? He'll be awfully stiff and cold when he wakes up.'

'He's not asleep, he's dead,' said Cynthia. 'And *please* keep your voice down, darling. There's a policeman walking up and down outside. I had to run out and clean up the mess quickly while his back was turned. It was quite horrid. You know how I hate that sort of thing.'

'Dead?' said Freddy. 'Are you sure? Perhaps he's just unconscious.'

He bent over unsteadily to peer at the motionless figure at his feet, then straightened up sharply.

'Oh, he's dead,' he said in surprise.

'That's what I'm trying to tell you,' said Cynthia. 'He died on the steps and I had to drag him inside. He was awfully heavy. And now I don't know what to do with him.'

'Why, call someone to take him away, surely? A doctor, perhaps? Or the police. Didn't you say there was a bobby just outside?'

'No!' exclaimed Cynthia. 'We can't call the police!'

'But why on earth not? You can't leave him here. He's not exactly ornamental, and he's blocking the doorway. The police will tidy him away nicely and soon it'll be as though he'd never been here, you'll see.'

'Don't be silly, Freddy. It's not funny. We need to get rid of him somehow, but without the police.'

Freddy's head was starting to spin, and he had the feeling there was something about the situation that he had not quite grasped fully.

'Look here, it's late,' he said. 'Perhaps we ought to leave him here and go and sleep on it. Then we can call someone tomorrow with a clear head, and they'll come and fix everything for you, and you won't have to think about it any more.'

But his mother was shaking her head vehemently.

'No!' she exclaimed. 'It's Mrs. Hanbury's day tomorrow, and you know what a dreadful old cat she is. If she turns up and finds a dead body here she'll tell your grandfather, and he'll be terribly cross with me. You know how long it took me to persuade him to let us use the house again after we held our "Rainbow Joy" party last year. I never meant everyone to start throwing paint at each other, but you remember the mess, and the bill for redecoration was rather high. It won't take much to set him off again. We must get Ticky out of here tonight.'

'But why don't you want the police?' said Freddy. 'And how did he die, anyway?' he added as an afterthought.

'Poison,' said Cynthia. 'At least, I think so.'

'Poison?' said Freddy. He stared, as the reality of the situation began to seep in slowly. 'You don't mean to say you killed him?'

'Don't be absurd, darling,' said Cynthia, although she looked a little uncomfortable. 'Why on earth would I kill Ticky?'

'But then how do you know?'

'Because he told me so himself. He was ill in the taxi on the way back, and when he got here he collapsed and was sick, and then he exclaimed, "Poisoned!" just like that, and died.'

'Good God!' said Freddy.

'Exactly,' said Cynthia. 'It was awfully sudden. We were out, a group of us, you see, for his birthday, and he ate *far* too much—between you and me it was rather revolting and I could hardly bear to watch it—and there was lots of wine and champagne, and that *dreadful* Van Leeuwen woman was there—I don't know who invited her—and of course then I was left without a lift and so I ended up in a taxi with Ticky. He spent half the journey drinking brandy out of the flask we gave him, because he didn't feel well, but it wasn't until he dropped dead outside the house that I found out just how ill he was. At any rate, it looks *most* suspicious that I was the last person to see him alive, so you see why we can't go to the police.'

'I don't actually,' said Freddy, who was struggling to keep up. 'Why *can't* we go to the police?'

'Why, because everyone will think I did it. I'll probably be arrested at the very least, or taken off for questioning, but I'm supposed to be going to Marjorie Belcher's reception tomorrow afternoon, and you *know* how strait-laced she is, and she's got Mr. Bickerstaffe in her thrall, and he'll probably give me the sack, and to be perfectly frank, darling, I could do with the money at the moment. Oh!' she exclaimed suddenly.

'What?' said Freddy.

'Nothing,' said Cynthia. 'I've just thought of something, that's all. Never mind. There's nothing I can do about it now. I shall just have to think about it later. In the meantime we have to get rid of Ticky. I suggest you go and leave him outside his front door. Then they'll think he died there and nobody need ever know he was here. It's only two hundred yards or so. I'll keep a look-out, if you like.'

'What do you mean, you suggest *I* leave him outside his front door?' said Freddy. 'What has all this to do with me?'

'Well, naturally, *I* can't carry him, darling. What an extraordinary idea! You must do it.'

'But—'

'Freddy, I simply insist. You know perfectly well—' She suddenly stopped and her eyes narrowed. 'Have you been *drinking*?' she said accusingly.

'No,' lied Freddy.

'You have, haven't you? I can always tell. Oh, Freddy, and just when I needed you. I feel you've let me down, somehow.'

'It was only—I couldn't help—Mungo insisted—look here, Mother, can't a man go for a perfectly innocent cocktail or two without—'

'Oh, never mind that now,' said Cynthia. 'We'll just have to do the best we can with what we've got. I only wish you'd had the sense to remain sober.'

Her tone was reproachful.

'Well, if you'd told me in advance you were planning to do away with someone, I might have,' said Freddy. 'Where's Father, by the way? Doesn't he usually dispose of your victims for you?'

'Don't be impertinent,' said Cynthia. 'As a matter of fact, your father *was* supposed to come this evening, but he had to take Mr. Fosse out for dinner at the last minute, and he said he would go straight back down to Richmond afterwards. Now, it's getting late and I'd rather like to go to bed, so let's get this over and done with instead of standing here talking. You pick him up and I'll just peep round the front door to make sure the policeman isn't still there.'

There is no doubt that Freddy had engaged in some, not to say many, morally dubious activities in his time; nonetheless, let the record show that he was not as a rule the sort of young man to aid and abet in the disposal of a dead body—at least, not while sober and in his right mind. However, his defences were always low when he was in drink, and in such a condition he was easily taken advantage of; moreover, Cynthia Pilkington-Soames was not a woman to be easily resisted at the best of times, since she had a tendency to talk incessantly until she got her own way. At present, therefore, Freddy's mind was fastening very hard on the only facts it would comfortably hold: the first being that there was a corpse cluttering up the entrance-hall, and the second, that he would not be allowed to go to bed until it had been tidied away. He sighed and resigned himself to the inevitable.

'Oh, very well, then,' he said. 'But I should like to make it clear that I do this on sufferance.'

He bent over Ticky and prepared to do as his mother said. According to his imagination, it ought to have been an easy matter to hoist the body up and fling it over his shoulder, but as he now discovered, picking up a corpse is not as easy as it sounds, since a dead weight is just that; and even fully sober it is unlikely that he would have been able to lift Ticky, who had not been a small man. After a certain amount of grappling that many would have considered not only unseemly but also highly disrespectful to the dead, Freddy stood back, panting.

'It's no good,' he said. 'I can't lift him.'

'But then what shall we do?' said Cynthia. 'Can you drag him instead?'

'What, and wake the entire street with the noise?' said Freddy. 'I might as well perch him on a barrel-organ and play it as we go. At least the money might pay for my bail.'

'Now you're being silly,' said Cynthia.

But talk of a barrel-organ had given Freddy an idea.

'What about a wheelbarrow?' he said. 'Where might we find such a thing?'

'I couldn't tell you,' said Cynthia. 'Not around here.'

'My wagon!' exclaimed Freddy.

'What?'

'You haven't thrown it away, have you? My little wagon, that I used to ride in. Do you remember? You had to pay the man when I ran over his dog. He was very annoyed.'

'Oh, that! I dare say it's still upstairs somewhere. Most likely in the attic. Why—'

But Freddy had already disappeared. He reappeared five minutes later, bearing a child's toy cart, and set it down on the floor. They regarded it dubiously.

'Will it hold his weight?' said Cynthia.

'We shall just have to try it,' said Freddy. 'You take his feet.'

'Oh, goodness,' said Cynthia, wrinkling her nose in distaste.

With some effort they managed to load Ticky into the wagon. His limbs were starting to stiffen, and he sat at an almost comical angle, his head tipped quizzically to one side as though he were wondering what was going on.

'Now, have a look outside. If there's no-one out there, I'll make a run for it,' said Freddy.

Cynthia opened the door and looked up and down the street.

'The policeman has just turned into Eaton Gate,' she said in a whisper.

'Go out and watch him,' said Freddy.

Cynthia hurried quietly down the steps and went to the corner of the street. She watched for a moment, then gesticulated wildly to signal that the coast was clear. Freddy pulled the wagon with difficulty over the threshold and bumped it down the steps, then stopped to rearrange Ticky, who had begun to slide out. He looked about him nervously, but saw nobody.

'Well, here goes,' he muttered.

The string on the little cart had long since frayed through, so there was nothing for it but to bend over and push. The wood creaked and buckled under Ticky's weight, but held, and the strange procession moved down the street, slowly at first, then faster. Cynthia was still standing at the corner, glancing about, as Freddy stopped to catch his breath.

'Go, darling,' she said, and Freddy did so. Now was the time to move as quickly as possible. Eaton Gate was deserted; presumably the policeman had turned into another street. Freddy braced himself and pushed Ticky across the road. It was hard work, for the wagon refused to maintain a straight course and was doing its best to veer off in any direction that took its fancy; moreover, every time it did so Ticky slid a little further out, and Freddy had to keep stopping to adjust him. He continued down Eaton Terrace and turned right into Caroline Terrace. Ticky lived not quite halfway along, at number 25. Freddy straightened the wagon carefully and, with one last burst of effort, bent almost double, broke into a run. He picked up such a turn of speed that he almost shot past the house, and had to stop suddenly. The wagon skidded and came to a standstill—unlike Ticky, who slid off and landed with a thud on the ground. Freddy winced and glanced around, for it seemed to him as though he must have drawn the attention of everyone in the street. Fortunately for him there was still nobody about, but Ticky was lying on the pavement for anyone to trip over who happened to be passing later. With a sigh, Freddy hefted him up under the arms and dragged him laboriously up the front path, where he propped him against the railings as best he could. Ticky was home at last.

Cynthia was on the landing in her dressing-gown when Freddy arrived back at the house, and seemed surprised to see him.

'Oh, it's you, darling,' she said over the banister. 'Did you have a good evening?'

Freddy opened his mouth to reply, but could think of none suitable.

'I suppose it's too late to get back to your rooms now,' she went on. 'You may have the blue room, but try and keep it tidy. Don't forget that Mrs. Hanbury is coming to do tomorrow, and she gets very upset if there's any mess. Goodnight.'

And with that she went into her room and shut the door, leaving Freddy standing in the hall, tired, dishevelled and with an incipient headache. At length he went upstairs and into the nearest bedroom, where he collapsed onto the bed, fully dressed, and was asleep within minutes.

CHAPTER THREE

THE SOUND OF singing filtered through into Freddy's brain, waking him by degrees. It was a low, droning, tuneless voice, which once heard was impossible to ignore. Freddy pulled a pillow over his head, but it was no good—the singing was just outside the door, and whoever it was seemed set fair to continue for the rest of the day, for the hymn, if that was what it was, appeared to have an infinite number of verses. Not a cheerful hymn about bountiful harvests and joyfulness, either; it was one of those paeans composed with the especial purpose of reminding one of one's inevitable doom. Something about being dragged to the judgment seat and dwelling in torment. As it happened, that was exactly how Freddy felt at that moment, for it seemed as though an entire orchestra had crept into his skull while he was asleep and begun to perform—except that each musician had decided to play a different tune at once. The percussion section was particularly enthusiastic, and he was almost sure that one of the percussionists had mistaken him for a bass drum, and was pounding him over the head rhythmically with a large mallet. There was no sleeping through such a racket, and so at last Freddy gave it up and groped for his watch. It must have stopped, he saw, for the hands pointed to half past ten. Then he remembered that it had been working perfectly well last night at eleven o'clock, and was seized with a terrible foreboding. He put the watch to his ear. It was still ticking. Freddy's editor, Mr. Bickerstaffe, had been expecting him at the *Clarion*'s offices at nine, having summoned him for an official dressing-down about his punctuality, and this was hardly a good beginning. He groaned. Just then there was a knock at the door.

'Beg pardon, Mr. Freddy,' said a voice. It was Mrs. Hanbury, the indefatigable singer of hymns, who let nothing stand in her way when there was dusting to be done—least of all young men who were still in bed long after they ought to be. Freddy sat up.

'It's all right, Mrs. H,' he managed, although the sudden movement had caused the brass section to begin improvising a polka. 'I'm going out now. You can have the room in five minutes.'

'No hurry, sir,' intoned Mrs. Hanbury, and began singing again.

Ten minutes later Freddy was out of the house and heading for Sloane Square as fast as his legs would carry him—which was not very fast, since for some reason he was aching all over and felt as though he had been in a fight. His memories of the night before were hazy, not to say almost non-existent, but this was too common an occurrence to worry him, and he expected it would all come back to him sooner or later. There was something about a dispute with Mungo over a taxi, he remembered.

He supposed Mungo must have won, since here he was in Belgravia rather than Fleet Street. Damn the fellow! But for him Freddy would not be in his present predicament, and would not be having to run halfway across London still wearing his evening things (indeed, his appearance was causing some amusement among passers-by). After another glance at his watch he decided not to go by the Underground, and instead leapt into a taxi, and by half past eleven finally arrived at the *Clarion*'s offices washed, dressed, and looking almost presentable. He was greeted without surprise by his colleagues in the news section, who knew his ways.

'Bickerstaffe's on the warpath,' one young man informed him. 'I hope you've got a good story, although I don't think anything less than bubonic plague will get you off the riot act.'

'Where is he?' said Freddy.

'In his office, with the Belcher. She's been spouting at him all morning. You'd better watch out. She's looking for victims. She caught Bill yesterday and forced him to sign a temperance pledge, and he's been in a foul mood ever since.'

'Bill?' said Freddy. He glanced across the room, where a freckled messenger boy could be seen licking stamps ferociously, a look of lowering fury upon his face.

'Caught him off guard,' said his colleague. 'If she asks me I'm going to say I've sprained my wrist and can't write.'

Freddy shuddered. Mrs. Marjorie Belcher was the current scourge of the *Clarion*, having made it her life's mission to effect the reform of society's morals by means of the organs of communication. In this she was aided immeasurably by the fact that she was the sister of Sir Aldridge Featherstone, the paper's owner, which gave her significant influence, and constant access to the news-room. She was the founder and leader of the Young Women's Abstinence Association, patron of at least two charities which sought to promote the adoption of a more virtuous way of life through healthy exercise, and a fervent believer in getting ten hours' sleep a night. She was almost fanatical in her enthusiasms, and while it ought to have been easy enough to avoid hearing about them merely by avoiding *her*, in reality she was so highly connected that it was almost impossible to attend any society party or reception without finding her also in attendance, or being button-holed by her at least once, for she was ever hopeful of persuading her acquaintances at the higher end of society to join one of her organizations. She had been haunting the news-room of late, and there were rumours among the staff that her brother, Sir Aldridge Featherstone himself, had been listening to her strictures, and was preparing to forbid the publication of the more scurrilous stories in which the *Clarion* tended to specialize. There was much dismay at the thought, for if the paper were to take a moral tone, then everybody knew it would quickly lose ground to its deadly rival, the *Herald*, and that would be the end of everything.

'Oh—here they come,' said the young man. 'Better look busy!'

A door at the end of the news-room opened as he spoke, and out came Mr. Bickerstaffe, accompanied by a large and officious-looking woman of middle age and respectable attire. Freddy slid quietly into his seat and affected to be busy with his notebook. The two moved slowly through the room, deep in conversation. Mr. Bickerstaffe was wearing his most ingratiating smile. As they approached, the woman could be heard saying:

'—and of course, it's no good at all if we cannot set an example ourselves. How are we to right the morals of the working classes if we cannot look to our own behaviour and pronounce it irreproachable? It is our duty, Mr. Bickerstaffe, to conduct ourselves at all times as though we were under constant observation—not only by our inferiors, but also by a Higher Power, one who will judge us when the final day comes, and find us all wanting—some of us more than others.'

This last was pronounced in a portentous tone.

'Oh, quite, Mrs. Belcher,' said Mr. Bickerstaffe.

They had now reached Freddy's desk. Freddy arranged some papers busily, and seemed to be hunting about for a pencil. Mr. Bickerstaffe caught sight of him and drew himself up.

'You,' he began, pointing a finger at Freddy.

But he was not allowed to continue, for Mrs. Belcher had not yet finished. She was looking about her at the reporters, who were all avoiding her eye and pretending to work.

'Perhaps some of your personnel might be persuaded to join us, in fact,' she said. 'If we can show the masses that even the fourth estate is working to support us, then they might be more likely to listen to what we have to say. Young man,' she said, addressing Freddy as he rose politely. 'You will not refuse, I am sure. I have no doubt that Mr. Bickerstaffe has told you of our cause—indeed, there is no more enthusiastic proponent of it than himself. For far too long our streets have been a hot-bed of criminality, vice, alcohol and sin. Our object is to cleanse the country of these diseases, before they take hold and society becomes wholly incurable.'

'A fine aim, certainly,' said Freddy, who was by no means recovered from the effects of at least one of the entries on her list, and was holding the edge of his desk to prevent himself from swaying. Mrs. Belcher looked at him more closely.

'What is your name? We have met before, have we not?' she said.

'Pilkington-Soames, madam,' he replied. 'I believe you know my mother.'

He was beginning to feel rather sick, and wanted nothing more than to go home and lie down again.

'Ah, yes!' exclaimed Mrs. Belcher. 'A very good woman, and wholly sympathetic to the cause. She was only too keen to come to my charity reception this afternoon. I shall look forward to seeing her at all our temperance meetings in future.'

At the mention of his mother, Freddy frowned as a flash of memory returned to him. He was almost sure she had been at the Eaton Terrace house last night, but presumably she had left before him that morning. Had there been a row of some sort? Mrs. Belcher had now moved on to another desk and was haranguing an elderly man for smoking. Mr. Bickerstaffe took advantage of her distraction to advance upon Freddy with a menacing look. Freddy braced himself for the worst, but before Mr. Bickerstaffe could begin he was interrupted by a lackey with an important message. He glanced at the paper and pursed his lips, then looked up at Freddy.

'One of your lot, I think,' he said.

'I beg your pardon, sir?' said Freddy.

'A dead body in Belgravia. Caroline Terrace. Maltravers, the name is. Know him? He's been found dead outside his next-door neighbour's house, and the police are hinting at foul play.'

At that there was a loud crash, as the memories returned all at once and Freddy sat down suddenly, accidentally sweeping the contents of his desk onto the floor as he did so.

'His *neighbour's* house? Number 25? Oh, good Lord,' he said.

There was some little bustle as several people started forward to pick up the mess.

'Are you quite all right, young man?' said Mrs. Belcher, alerted by the noise. 'You look a little unwell, I must say.'

Freddy was staring straight ahead, white in the face, as an image of himself, wheeling the dead body of Ticky Maltravers from his mother's house to Caroline Terrace in a child's toy wagon, danced through his mind in all its magnificence and glory. He put his head in his hands and groaned.

'I need a drink,' he said.

'Well, really!' said Mrs. Belcher, taken aback.

'You don't look well, old chap,' said the young man at the next desk.

'I take it you knew him,' said Mr. Bickerstaffe.

Freddy pulled himself together with some effort.

'No—at least, not well,' he said. 'He was a friend of my mother's.'

'Ah, yes, your mother,' said Mr. Bickerstaffe. 'Where is she this morning, by the way? She hasn't sent in her copy yet and we need it by three for the six o'clock edition.'

'I expect she's hovering excitedly around Scotland Yard, trying to get a glimpse of the corpse,' said the young man.

'Sorry, Freddy,' he said hurriedly, as Freddy glared at him. 'Just my little joke.'

'You said the police are talking about foul play,' said Freddy to Mr. Bickerstaffe. 'Does that mean they suspect murder?'

'Can't say from this,' said Mr. Bickerstaffe, looking at the message. 'It just says here there are some suspicious circumstances. Jolliffe,' he said to the young man, 'you go along there and find out what's going on.'

'Do you mind if I go instead, sir?' said Freddy. 'After all, I did know him. A little, anyway,' he added hastily.

Mr. Bickerstaffe stared at him doubtfully.

'But I'm supposed to be having a word with you,' he said.

'Excuse me, am I to understand that Mr. Pilkington-Soames was a friend of this unfortunate person?' said Mrs. Belcher. 'Why, there's no wonder he looks so unwell. It must be a terrible shock. And to offer to write the story, too, at such a moment! That's very spirited of you, young man. Mr. Bickerstaffe, the country needs more young people such as this. Too often these days we see youth so easily overcome by the slightest blow, but Mr. Pilkington-Soames here is a perfect demonstration of what a stout heart can do.'

'Thank you, madam,' said Freddy bravely. 'I hope I understand my duty.'

Jolliffe at the next desk let out a snigger, which he covered with a cough.

'You do look very pale, however,' went on Mrs. Belcher. 'Perhaps you ought to go home and recover.'

'No, there's no need for that,' said Freddy. 'But I should like to go and cover the story, if you don't mind, sir. After all, I did know him a little, and I know some of his pals very well. I rather think I can make something of it, if you'll let me.'

'Oh, very well,' said Mr. Bickerstaffe grudgingly. 'But don't think you're off the hook just yet. Well, what are you waiting for? Get along.'

Freddy needed no further encouragement. He wished Mrs. Belcher a respectful good morning and headed for the door. He needed to find out what the police knew, and then speak to his mother.

CHAPTER FOUR

INSPECTOR ENTWISTLE STOOD outside the front door of number 24, Caroline Terrace, in close conference with his sergeant, Bird, and another man carrying a little black case that announced him immediately as a doctor. The inspector was a man whom nobody could have picked out in a crowd, and that was the way he liked it. For twenty years he had dedicated himself to his job almost to the exclusion of all else, and he regretted it not for a moment. His calling was the law, and the law he meant to uphold, come what may. Sergeant Bird, more affable and less unbending, had nonetheless worked with his superior for some years now, and knew how to manage him, and the two men rubbed along fairly well for the most part. They now listened earnestly to what the doctor had to tell them about the strange events of that morning.

Nicholas Maltravers had been discovered outside the house of his next-door neighbour at number 25, Caroline Terrace at eight o'clock, when the maid had come out to scrub the step. The young woman had screamed loudly at the unexpected sight of a dead man in full evening-dress propped up against her nice, clean railings, and the noise had brought out her elderly mistress, who was not a little displeased at having her breakfast interrupted by such a row. Miss Fosdyke was made of sterner stuff than her maid; she recognized Ticky immediately and sent the girl round to fetch Weaver, Ticky's manservant. Weaver went pale at the sight, wrung his hands and summoned a doctor, and together they carried Ticky into his own house and laid him as best they could on his bed. The doctor had attended Ticky many times and knew him well, and his suspicions were very soon aroused by one or two little circumstances that caused him to frown. He questioned Weaver closely about where his master had been last night, and whether he had been in any way unwell recently, and then announced that he could not think of issuing a death certificate until the police had been called. A young constable was sent along, but swiftly saw that it was a serious matter and that more help would be needed. He was now engaged in keeping an eye on the small crowd of people who had gathered outside number 24 to watch proceedings, while Entwistle and Bird heard what the doctor had to say.

'So you see what I mean about the traces,' Dr. Spillman was saying. 'The unnatural position of the body first gave me pause, since it was propped up most awkwardly against the railings. His lower parts were not quite touching the ground, while his right foot had been jammed against the doorstep as though to hold him in place. That puzzled me slightly, but my suspicions were not fully confirmed until after we'd moved him and carried him up to bed. That's when I noticed traces of vomit around his mouth, although there was no mess where he was found. Then when I examined the rest of him I saw that the heels of his shoes were worn and scraped, and that the hems on his trousers were also a little frayed and dirty, just as though he'd been dragged.'

'You think someone put him there, then?' said Entwistle.

'Yes. At first glance it looked as though he had been taken ill, and had collapsed against the railings and slid down into a sitting position—and I expect that is what we were meant to think. But when I examined him at just before nine this morning, it was clear that rigor was well advanced, and he had obviously been dead some time—perhaps as much as ten or twelve hours. However, Miss Fosdyke's maid says that she just glanced out into the street at half past eleven last night when she locked up, and he was not there then. It's not certain, of course, but I think someone put him here when he had already begun to stiffen, and arranged him to look as if he had died outside the house. I do beg your pardon, inspector—had I been thinking more clearly I should, of course, have insisted on his being left where he was found, but my mind was on other things this morning, and I had no particular reason to suspect foul play initially. I'm afraid you'll just have to take my word for it about his original position.'

'Hmm,' said Entwistle. 'And you're sure there was no heart trouble?'

'None at all. I'd attended him for years, and his heart was as sound as a bell. He had one or two other conditions, but none that would cause him to collapse suddenly and die in the street. I can't say what killed him, but it certainly bears further investigation, don't you think?'

'Perhaps,' said Entwistle non-committally.

The doctor prepared to leave.

'I'd like to stay and speak to the police surgeon when he arrives, but I'm already late for several appointments,' he said. 'Here's my card, anyway. I shall be back in my office by three if he wants to speak to me.'

And with a brisk nod, he hurried off. Inspector Entwistle was already looking about him.

'So, if this Maltravers was brought here, where was he brought from?' he said. 'And how was he killed?'

'You think it was murder, then, sir?' said Sergeant Bird.

'Can't say until Ingleby gets here and takes a look at him,' said Entwistle. 'But in the meantime there's no harm in scouting about a bit.' He went to peer at the pavement outside number 25. 'Ah,' he said. 'See here. Yes; unmistakable traces of black shoe-polish and leather, I should say. He was certainly dragged. But the trace only starts here in the middle of the street. He wasn't dragged all the way, then.'

'What if he collapsed here in the street, and someone moved him?' suggested Bird.

'Why would they do that and not call for help?'

'Perhaps they thought he was drunk.'

'Possible, I suppose. Although this doctor chappie seems to think he was already stiff when he was propped up. You couldn't drag a dead body and not notice he was dead.'

'True enough,' conceded the sergeant. 'But why did they put him outside number 25 when he lives at number 24? Was it deliberate?'

'I've no idea,' said Entwistle. He was still looking about him thoughtfully.

'Perhaps someone wanted to play a nasty joke on Miss Fosdyke,' said Bird.

'There must be some reason for it,' said Entwistle. 'Unless whoever it was dumped him there by mistake. We'll need to speak to this manservant—what's his name?—Weaver, and find out what his gentleman was doing last night. He's in the house, yes?'

'Prostrate with grief,' said the sergeant resignedly. 'Couldn't get a word out of him. I said we'd come back.'

'Well, he'd better not suffer too long. We haven't time for fits of the vapours. Hallo, who's this? Stay back, sir. Police.'

He was addressing a slightly dishevelled-looking young man, who had just pushed through the little crowd and past the protesting police constable, and who now paused to look about him with interest, as though he had all the time in the world.

'What do you think you're doing?' said Sergeant Bird. Freddy bestowed an ingratiating smile upon the two policemen.

'Sorry, I was just stopping to get a whiff of the atmosphere, and all that, what? The readers like a bit of local colour with their corpses. Press,' he explained. 'Pilkington-Soames, here on behalf of the *Clarion*. Here's my card. I'm afraid it's a little battered and wrinkled around the edges, from the time I went to speak to Mr. Bartholomew—you know, the trade union leader—during the dock-workers' strike, and his Doberman Pinscher took a liking to it and dropped it into the Regent's Canal. Luckily a passing barge-man fished it out for me, but it's never been the same since. I prefer smaller dogs, myself. There's something not quite natural about a dog that's so tall it can look one straight in the eye, don't you think?'

'The *Clarion*?' said Inspector Entwistle, fastening upon the one salient detail of this speech. 'We've got nothing for you at present. Come to the Yard later, if you must, but don't bother us now. Ah, here's Ingleby,' he said, as the little police surgeon arrived. 'I want a word with him.'

He hurried off, and Sergeant Bird was left to deal with the press.

'Friendly chap, isn't he?' said Freddy.

'He hasn't got time for trivialities,' said Bird, assessing the young man with a practised eye.

'I might take exception to being called a triviality,' said Freddy. 'Luckily for you, I have an extraordinarily thick skin, so I'll forgive you on this occasion.'

'Good of you,' said the sergeant. 'But he's right, you know. There's nothing doing here at the moment. You'd be better off waiting until we've finished.'

'Are you familiar with the word "deadline?"' said Freddy.

'Something to do with fishing, isn't it?' said Bird.

'Not exactly. It's a line beyond which stands a door marked "The Boot." Which is why I fully intend to stand here and talk at you until you give me something I can put in the paper. Come now,' he went on, in his most persuasive manner. 'You wouldn't want to see me, my wife and my five children out on the street by the end of the week, purely because I couldn't get four hundred words to my editor in time for the six o'clock edition, now, would you?'

'I wouldn't if I believed a word of it, sir,' said Bird comfortably. 'But you heard what Inspector Entwistle said. And anyway, there's nothing to tell. A gentleman was found dead outside his next-door neighbour's house, and we don't yet know how it happened.'

'His next-door neighbour's house, eh? That's interesting. Any idea how he got there? Had he gone there for tea, or something?'

'No. He was found there early this morning, having somehow arrived there during the night.'

'But there must be something you're not telling me, sergeant,' said Freddy. 'I mean to say, you wouldn't be here now if there weren't something suspicious about his death. What is it? A gunshot wound to the temple? A dagger to the heart? A mysterious note, smelling faintly of perfume, clutched in the dead man's hand?'

'Nothing so exciting as that, I'm afraid,' said Bird, amused despite himself. 'The only mystery at present is how he came to be where he was, as it rather looks as if someone put him there—at least, that's what his doctor says. But we don't know who, and we don't know how.'

'No witnesses, I suppose?' said Freddy, as casually as possible.

'Not so far. This is a quiet street and it's unlikely anybody was out and about in the middle of the night. And as for the dead man, he certainly wasn't shot or stabbed, but we won't know how he *did* die until there has been a post-mortem examination. And now that's all I can tell you.'

'Splendid. And in return I shall tell *you* that I knew the dead man—slightly, at any rate.'

'Did you, indeed?' said Bird with sudden interest.

'Yes, I thought that might get you. As a matter of fact, I'm surprised you haven't heard of him yourself—or are you one of these types who professes not to read the society pages?'

'I may have perused them on occasion,' admitted Bird cautiously.

'Then you must have heard of Ticky Maltravers, surely?'

'The name does sound familiar. Is this the same gentleman?'

'The very same. Now, listen; I'm in a spot of trouble with my editor, and he's put me on to this story, and if I can steal a march on the competition—the *Herald* in particular—then I'll be back in his good books. What do you say to a little exchange of information? You tell me what you know—or at least, as much as you can say without ruining your case—and I'll tell you anything I find out. A sort of *quid pro quo*, what?'

'I can't promise anything,' said Bird. 'The inspector's not too keen on that kind of thing.'

'Doesn't trust the press, eh?' said Freddy. 'Very wise, as a general rule. I, however, am a man of unimpeachable morals and ironclad honour, who would never dream of publishing a story without your say-so.'

'That remains to be seen,' said Bird. 'As I said, we can't be certain there's any mystery at all, yet. I've told you all I know, and if you can get four hundred words out of that then you're a better man than I am.'

'Oh, I shall pad it out somehow,' said Freddy, with a wave of the hand. 'It's rather a gift of mine. I once spent six hundred words describing the hat-ribbons of an abandoned wife who killed her children and then herself, and everyone said it was one of the most moving and tragic things I'd ever written. So, let's take that as agreed, shall we? I shall go off and write my little piece, then you shall read it and see that I am exactly what I purport to be, and can be relied upon not to transform a dull news story into a work of vulgar fiction—although you must allow for a *little* poetic licence, naturally—and then we shall become friends and entrust one another with such little tidbits of useful information that might happen to come our way.'

'I make no promises,' said Sergeant Bird again. 'Now, you're standing where you ought not to, so you'd better go and write your story. No hat-ribbons here, I'm afraid.'

He then went off to speak to the constable, leaving Freddy to think about what he had learnt. Despite his apparent insouciance, he was in fact deeply relieved that the police had not arrested him on the spot as soon as he had arrived. They had evidently not found any witnesses to the disposal of Ticky's body yet, and Freddy trusted fervently that they never would, and that by ingratiating himself with the police he would throw them off the scent. The inspector did not look like much of a prospect, but this sergeant seemed a friendly enough sort, and would perhaps let him know what was going on with the investigation. Ever since the memory of last night had come back to him, Freddy had been kicking himself at his own stupidity, and was at present highly displeased with his mother for having taken advantage of him in his weakened state, for he had no desire to run afoul of the law, and was quite certain he would never have agreed to what she had asked of him had he been fully *compos mentis* at the time. But was Cynthia right when she said Ticky had been poisoned? How did she know? Or was she being over-dramatic, as usual? If she was right, then the police were bound to find it out, and then they would start asking awkward questions about where everybody had been last night. Of course, Ticky's death was nothing to do with Freddy, but he suspected the police would not look too kindly upon his half-unwitting interference in the affair.

The thing to do now was to find his mother, and quickly. But where was she? Just then, Freddy remembered his conversation with Marjorie Belcher, who had mentioned that Cynthia was supposed to be attending her charity reception at Sir Aldridge Featherstone's house that afternoon. He would have to run her to earth there. At any rate, he seemed safe from arrest for the moment. Two men were now emerging from number 24, bearing a covered figure on a stretcher. The little crowd which had gathered in the street now became very excited, and surged forward in an attempt to get a better view, as Sergeant Bird and the ineffectual police constable tried to hold them back. Freddy took the opportunity to melt away. The reception was at three, he seemed to remember. He would have some lunch to restore his faculties, then he would go and find his mother and give her a piece of his mind.

Chapter Five

AT TWELVE O'CLOCK that same day, Nancy Beasley was lying in bed at her house in Charles Street, a cold compress on her forehead, dictating a letter to her secretary, an attractive and competent young woman of twenty-five.

'Let's see,' she said. 'Shall I start "Dear Lady Featherstone?" Or shall I risk "Constance?" It's so difficult to know what to do in these circumstances. Obviously one doesn't want to offend, but if I give her the full title I've as good as admitted that I know she's snubbing me. What do you think, Ann?'

Ann Chadwick thought for a moment.

'It is difficult,' she conceded. 'And I'm not sure I know the answer, since I haven't seen the two of you together lately. How was she the last time you saw her?'

'Oh, the same as before—quite cut me dead when she saw me. And in public, too. Only think of the humiliation! It's too bad of her. And it's not as though I did it on purpose. How was I to know she was throwing her beastly party on the same day as mine? Just a tiny little *faux pas* and she's been holding a grudge against me for months now. And after all I put myself through to get in with her in the first place—all those charitable committees I've inveigled myself onto, and all the things I've had to hide from Marjorie Belcher, who simply can't imagine that a person might want to have a little fun once in a while. I don't suppose for one second that Constance is as virtuous as she makes herself out to be, but with a sister-in-law like Mrs. Belcher she can pretend as much as she likes to be holier than thou, and nobody doubts it for a second. I'll bet no-one asked *her* a lot of awkward questions about her views on drink before they let her on the board of trustees. Hateful woman! I can't bear people who won't forgive and forget.'

'If you can't bear Lady Featherstone, then surely it doesn't matter what you call her,' said Ann. 'And there must be other charities who would be glad of your help?'

'Silly girl, I don't give a fig about the charities,' said Nancy pettishly. 'It's the *look* of the thing that's important. Of course I must pretend to be her friend. Why, you know perfectly well that she throws *the* most important parties. One simply has to be seen at them, or one might as well retire to the wilds of Scotland and take up fishing. The invitations will be going out to her Christmas ball soon, and everyone who's anyone will be there, so I can't possibly let her freeze me out, as I'd simply die if she didn't invite me, and Cynthia would never let me hear the last of it. Think of everyone gloating over it if she put it in the *Clarion*! I should never be able to hold my head up in public again.'

'In that case, I think the best choice would be the formal title.'

'You think I ought to grovel?' said Nancy, wrinkling her nose.

'Perhaps it might be safest. Oh, but it's Mrs. Belcher's reception this afternoon,' said Ann, as a thought struck her. 'Lady Featherstone will be there, won't she? Perhaps you might leave the letter for now, and see whether you can't try and thaw things a little in person first.'

'Now there's an idea,' said Nancy. 'Do you know, I believe you're right. I shall go to the reception and be charming and delightful to Mrs. Belcher, and then Constance will have no choice but to acknowledge me, because she's the one who'll look bad if she doesn't. She might be cool, but she certainly can't ignore me, and that will be a start, at any rate. You'll back me up, won't you, Ann? Oh, Denis, darling,' she said to her husband, who entered the room then, 'I've just had the cleverest idea. I'm going to work on Constance Featherstone at the reception this afternoon before I reply to that frosty letter of hers about the opera recital. If I suck up to Marjorie Belcher and pretend to be dreadfully enthusiastic about her silly temperance association, Constance won't be able to snub me, or she'll lose face in front of everyone. What do you think?'

Denis Beasley and Ann Chadwick exchanged glances of understanding, unseen by Nancy on the bed.

'I don't know why you're so bothered about that woman,' he said. 'She's not worth half the attention you give her. Hallo, Ann. Did you and Larry have a nice time last night?'

'Yes, thank you,' said Ann.

'They had a better time of it than we did, I imagine,' said Nancy. 'They went to the theatre to see that new play we liked the look of, while we were all suffering through a positively interminable evening with Ticky. You must promise me never again, darling.'

'It wasn't my idea,' said Denis. 'I can't bear the fellow. He practically drips oil.'

'Wasn't it a nice evening?' said Ann.

'Far too loud for my taste,' said Nancy. 'I prefer a smaller, quieter party. Still, at least he seemed to like the flask.'

'Oh, I'm glad,' said Ann. 'I almost decided on the pocket-watch, but then I remembered that he prefers a wrist-watch.'

'I never know what to buy people,' said Nancy. 'I'm lucky I have you for all that sort of thing. Just plump this pillow up for me, would you darling?'

Ann did as she was told, and Nancy sighed.

'I did think Captain Atherton might have had more to say for himself. He must have some thrilling tales to tell about life in the jungle, but he didn't seem inclined to indulge us last night. And Sarah Bendish was there, looking sick as usual. I don't know what she's got to complain about—she seems to have a perfectly comfortable life, but she insists on moping about with a face like melting wax. I'm sorry, darling,' she said to Ann. 'I know you're marrying into the family, and I'm sure she's a perfectly delightful woman, but I only wish she'd cheer up a little.'

'Now, Nancy,' began Denis, but got no further before the telephone-bell rang. Ann Chadwick rose to answer the instrument, which stood on a little table by the bed.

'It's Mrs. Pilkington-Soames,' she said to Nancy, who removed her cold compress and took the receiver.

'Cynthia, darling,' she said. 'Ghastly night, wasn't it?'

She listened to the excitable voice at the other end of the line, and her eyes grew round.

'What?' she exclaimed. 'Are you sure? But how?' She was silent as the voice chattered on. 'Oh, I see. You weren't there? Then who told you? Yes, yes, of course. Well, how simply extraordinary! I'll tell Denis immediately. Yes, I imagine you are in a hurry. You'll be there this afternoon, won't you? Good; you shall tell me more about it then. Goodbye.'

She replaced the receiver and looked at Denis and Ann, who were regarding her with the greatest of curiosity.

'Ticky's dead!' she said, and then, as they exclaimed, went on, 'Cynthia says he collapsed outside his house last night. She's just heard it from the people at the paper.'

'Heart attack?' suggested Denis.

'They don't know, but there seems to be some suggestion that he might not have died of natural causes. The police have been called, and there's going to be a post-mortem examination.'

'Goodness!' said Ann. 'Does that mean they'll want to come and ask you questions?'

'I dare say,' said Nancy. 'What a bore. Marjorie Belcher won't be any too pleased at having anyone from her charities mixed up in a police investigation.'

'I suppose not,' said Ann. 'It sounds rather unpleasant.'

They all looked at one another.

'Still, he's dead,' said Denis at last, and he did not look particularly unhappy.

'I wonder whether anyone else knows,' said Nancy, picking up the telephone-receiver again.

'If they don't *now*, they soon will,' Denis said quietly to Ann, who smiled.

CAPTAIN MAURICE ATHERTON put down the telephone and stared into space for a long moment. It was impossible to read the expression on his lean, tanned face, but it was obvious that he was thinking hard. At length, he stretched his hand out and rang a little bell, which was soon answered by a man-servant.

'Mahomet,' he said. 'I've just heard the most extraordinary piece of news.'

The manservant waited politely.

'Maltravers is dead.'

'Is that so, sir?'

'Yes. Collapsed outside his house last night.'

He paused. Mahomet waited, knowing his master well.

'I won't say it's not a relief,' went on Atherton. 'The man was a foul pestilence, right enough. But they don't know how he died, and it looks as though the police have been called. They'll start poking around, no doubt.'

'Do you suppose they will find anything, sir?' said Mahomet.

'That's the question, isn't it? At least while he was alive there was no danger of—'

He stopped, and turned to the other, looking him search-ingly in the eye.

'If only one could get into the house,' he said. 'I'd go myself, but that wretched servant of his was under instructions not to let me in after we nearly came to blows last time, and I don't suppose anything's changed just because he's dead.'

'Do you wish me to go and see what I can find out?' said Mahomet.

'Would you? Will his man speak to you?'

'I do not think so. He has made disparaging remarks about my brown skin in the past,' said Mahomet with perfect equanimity. 'But there are—other means of finding out what one wants to know.'

Atherton smiled.

'You're a wily one,' he said. 'I have no doubt that you'll find a way.'

'There is always a way,' said Mahomet.

'Very well. You know what to look for,' said Atherton.

Mahomet gave a little bow and left the room, and Captain Atherton was left to consider his next move.

———————

AT TWO O'CLOCK that afternoon, Lady Bendish was gazing mournfully out of the window at her house in Curzon Street, while her son walked up and down the room impatiently. Larry Bendish was dark-haired and handsome, and resembled his mother greatly, although there was an inner energy to him which his mother lacked, and which came from his father.

'You say they don't know how he died?' said Larry.

'No,' said Lady Bendish, without turning away from the window.

'Then there'll have to be a post-mortem examination. That's what they do when there's a suspicious death. They cut them open and poke about, looking for signs of what might have caused it.'

'Please, darling,' said Lady Bendish, with a pained expression. 'Must we?'

'Sorry, Mother,' said Larry. 'It's rather fascinating, that's all.'

'Anyway, I don't suppose there's the slightest mystery to it,' said Lady Bendish. 'He ate far too much and it was probably some sort of apoplexy. I noticed he was pink in the face and breathing heavily when we all left Babcock's, but thought nothing of it at the time. Perhaps Cynthia Pilkington-Soames will know something. They went off together in a taxi, so she must have been the last person to see him alive.'

'I hope you're right about the cause of death,' said Larry. 'It's just queer that the police seem to think it was foul play.' He threw his mother a look which she did not see. 'What shall you do now?' he went on lightly, as though there were nothing in the question.

'Do?' she said. 'What is there to do? We must wait, that's all.'

'Wait for what?' he said quickly. 'The police to come? But surely this is the time to act, before—'

She looked at him in surprise.

'Before what?' she said. There was the slightest touch of alarm in her tone, and he dared not go on. He looked at the floor.

'Nothing. I just thought you might want to go to his house and pay your respects in person,' he said.

'To whom? To that manservant of his? What could I say?'

'I don't know. That you're very sorry, and that you've come to collect—the thing you left at his house.'

'What thing?' She was even more alarmed now. 'Really, darling, I have no idea what you're talking about. I haven't left anything at his house. There's nothing at all—' here she broke off, then set her jaw. 'Why should you think Ticky's death affects me in any way?'

'I don't,' he said. 'Not if you say it doesn't.'

'Well, it doesn't,' she said firmly. 'I'm sorry he's gone, of course, but it's not as though he was a close friend, and I won't pretend to mourn him. We shall just have to wait and see what happens.'

Larry sighed. There was no use in trying to continue the conversation, since it was perfectly obvious that she had no intention of being open with him.

'Very well, then, let's wait,' he said. 'I only hope that whatever does happen isn't too awful.'

He then left the room, and she gazed out of the window once more.

'I dare say something will turn up,' she murmured to herself, with furrowed brow.

———

BLANCHE VAN LEEUWEN examined her face from all angles in the looking-glass. The new face-powder she had bought from the exclusive and costly shop on Bond Street was a most flattering shade of peach, she decided, and made a mental note to order some more. Her daughter, Amelia Drinkwater, sat curled up in an armchair and observed her dispassionately.

'You don't seem particularly upset,' she said.

'I'm not upset at all,' said Blanche. 'In fact, I'm as light as air. He was such a bore. It was quite a torture to have to sit next to him for the whole evening.'

'Why did you go, then?'

Blanche opened her pale blue eyes wide.

'Because one does, of course. And the Pilkington-Soames woman was going, and I couldn't let her see I was at all bothered by those beastly lies she wrote about me. But the food was dreadful—you know how I hate eating in the evening—and I had to watch him shovelling the stuff into his mouth as though he hadn't been fed in a week. I'm certain he ordered the most expensive things deliberately, just because he knew he wouldn't be paying for it. Well, he did pay for it in the end, didn't he?'

Here she gave a heartless laugh. Amelia made no comment, but plucked at a loose piece of thread on her sleeve.

'Why was Ticky so popular, anyway?' she said after a moment. 'I never liked him myself. He *oozed*.'

'What an extraordinary word, darling,' said Blanche, arranging a curl of hair artfully across her cheek.

'Oh, but it's true. He was rather ghastly. And he didn't smile so much as leer.'

'One oughtn't to speak ill of the dead like that, my sweet. If nothing else, it's terribly unladylike.'

'But you just did it yourself! You said he was a bore.'

'And so he was, I can't deny it. But let's not talk about him any more. I'm sick to death of the subject.'

'All right, then, I won't if you won't,' said Amelia. 'By the way, when's Andrew back from Singapore? Monday, isn't it? Do you want me to come with you to meet him?'

'Oh, didn't I tell you? I had a telegram from him this morning. The business is taking longer than he thought, so he won't be back for another month at least, and perhaps more.'

'Then why don't we go and join him? You keep promising me that we'll travel one day. And then it's not far from Singapore to Australia. Can't we go, Mummy? I should love to see Sydney, and all the places you've told me about.'

'Certainly not,' said Blanche. 'I have no intention of going back, so there's no use in asking me about it.'

Amelia knew when her mother had made up her mind.

'But won't you be bored without Andrew for another month?' she said.

'Oh, I can always find something to entertain myself,' said Blanche, a satisfied smile playing around her pretty mouth. She glanced at the clock. 'Speaking of which, isn't it time you were going out to this reception of yours?'

'I'm waiting for Ann and Larry,' said Amelia. 'They said they'd call for me, but they're late.'

'Ann and Larry?' said Blanche, stopping what she was doing for a second, and turning to look at her daughter. 'You will be all right, won't you darling?'

'Of course I will,' said Amelia.

'I mean, your heart isn't broken, or anything?'

'Don't be silly. It was just a childish thing. Ann is my pal, and she and Larry will make a marvellous couple,' said Amelia stoutly. 'I shall sit in the front row at their wedding and cheer them on. Figuratively speaking, of course.' She looked up at her mother. 'You're wrinkling your brow, by the way. You know you oughtn't to do that. Are you worried about me? I told you, there's no need.'

'I'm not worried about you, darling—or anything else for that matter,' said Blanche, as the doorbell rang and Amelia jumped up. 'After all, I'm sure nobody will be interested in a few old newspapers,' she added in a murmur.

'What?' said Amelia, throwing on her scarf.

'Nothing,' said Blanche. 'Now, off you go, and have a lovely time.'

'It will probably be deadly dull,' said Amelia, and went out.

CHAPTER SIX

FREDDY ARRIVED LATE at Mrs. Belcher's reception, having gone home for a bite of lunch and unaccountably fallen asleep afterwards, so it was gone four o'clock when he arrived at Sir Aldridge Featherstone's mansion in Grosvenor Square. The first thing he saw on being ushered into the grand salon was his mother and Nancy Beasley, in earnest conversation with Marjorie Belcher herself. Cynthia spotted him immediately, but affected not to and went on talking, and he narrowed his eyes in exasperation. An enthusiastic woman with a collection box advanced upon him, and within five minutes he had spent seventeen shillings and ninepence on raffle tickets and other donations, and had narrowly avoided being tricked into signing a temperance pledge. He escaped the clutches of the enthusiastic woman, and went across to a long table, spread with a white cloth, behind which two or three slightly defeated-looking young women of the lower classes were standing, waiting to serve him tea. Several others of their kind were standing in a gaggle in one corner, looking and evidently feeling out of place, having been given their tea separately in the less valuable china. They bore patiently the stares of the guests and the loud remarks of the charity ladies, as they were pointed out at every opportunity as shining examples of what a pledge to abstain from drink could do. One of them, Freddy noticed, was eyeing an unattended silver teaspoon with interest.

Since it was obvious that his mother would be engaged for some time to come, he made a bee-line for someone he recognized. It was Larry Bendish, who was standing in conversation with Ann Chadwick and another young woman.

'Hallo, Freddy,' said Larry. 'What are you doing here? Oughtn't you to be plugging away at a typewriter? Or did they send you to write a story about the evils of the demon drink? Dreadful bore, this sort of thing, but I promised my mother I'd come, and so here I am. You know Ann, don't you? Of course you do.'

Freddy said what was proper, and then Ann said:

'Have you met Amelia?'

Freddy turned to see a girl with neat brown hair and wide, pale blue eyes, and was instantly smitten.

'Amelia Drinkwater. Pleased to meet you,' said Amelia.

'Oh, I say, what?' said Freddy idiotically, and forgot to introduce himself.

'I expect you've heard about Ticky,' said Larry Bendish.

Freddy closed his mouth with a snap and pulled himself together.

'Ticky Maltravers?' he said, as though he knew several Tickys. 'Yes, the paper sent me along there this morning.'

'And what did you find out?' said Amelia with the greatest curiosity. 'Did you speak to the police? Do they really suspect foul play?'

'They wouldn't say,' said Freddy. 'I don't expect they know themselves, yet. They'll have to do a post-mortem to find out how he died.'

'I understand he dropped dead outside his own house,' said Larry.

'As a matter of fact, it was the house next door,' said Freddy. 'He didn't make it as far as home.'

'But why were the police called at all?' said Amelia. 'I mean, who decided his death was suspicious?'

'Ticky's doctor, I gather. He—er—seemed to think the body had been moved, and thought it needed looking into,' said Freddy uncomfortably.

'He was moved after he died, do you mean?' said Larry in surprise. 'Why would someone do that? And where was he moved from?'

'I couldn't say,' replied Freddy, for to tell the truth was obviously impossible.

'Well, it's all very mysterious,' said Amelia. 'I shall be poring over the newspapers to find out what happens next. I do love a good murder.'

'Murder!' said Ann, laughing. 'Why, Amelia, I believe your imagination is running away with you. What on earth makes you think he was murdered?'

'I have an instinct for these things. Just you watch—I'll bet that some time soon we'll read that they've found out he was poisoned or something, and then the police will be all over the place, and Mummy will become even more impossible than she is now. She was at Babcock's with him last night, for his birthday,' she explained, in reply to Freddy's questioning look.

'Really? So was my mother,' he said.

'And mine,' said Larry.

'How funny!' said Amelia. 'Then we already have three murder suspects. Not that I believe for a moment that my mother would kill anyone, of course.'

Freddy said nothing, since he could not speak quite so confidently about Cynthia.

'It's five, if you include Mr. and Mrs. Beasley,' said Ann. 'And Captain Atherton was there, too—you know, the explorer.'

'You mean the one who discovered that lost tribe in the Amazon jungle?' said Amelia. 'Goodness! Well, that makes six. I expect one of them put something in his food. I wonder which of them it was.'

'I don't really suppose it was any of them—or anybody at all, in fact,' said Ann. 'And I don't know that it's a good idea to be talking about murder at this stage. There might be a perfectly ordinary explanation for what happened, and we don't want people gossiping and pointing fingers at innocent people, now, do we?'

'How sensible you are!' said Amelia. 'No wonder Mrs. Beasley can't do without you.'

'She'll have to, soon,' said Larry. 'I can't do without her either, and husbands come first.'

'When is it to be?' said Amelia. 'And won't it feel strange to move out of that enormous house in Charles Street, and into a little place of your own?'

'Ann prefers a smaller house, don't you, Ann?' said Larry. 'It'll be easier for her to look after, since we won't have a great deal of money to start with, and shall have to struggle along for a little while.'

'I don't mind that,' said Ann cheerfully. 'I've always been poor, and I'm used to making do.'

She and Amelia began to talk of weddings and gowns, and other subjects of interest only to the female mind, and Freddy's eye wandered away for a moment—fortunately for him, for he just then saw his mother, who was quite obviously trying to sidle out of the room without being seen. Excusing himself quickly, he ran out after her, and caught up with her at the bottom of the marble staircase.

'Where do you think you're going?' he said.

She started guiltily.

'Oh, there you are, darling!' she said. 'I was just about to go outside and have a cigarette. You know how Mrs. Belcher disapproves of smoking, but there are some things one simply can't give up, however good the cause.'

'All right, then, I'll come with you,' he said.

'There's no need for that. In fact, I'd far rather you didn't. I need someone to distract her before she notices I'm missing. I'll only be five minutes.'

She made as if to leave, but Freddy caught hold of her arm.

'Not so fast,' he said. 'If you think I'm letting you run off, you're very much mistaken. I want a word with you.'

Cynthia pouted.

'You're being very tiresome,' she said, then sighed as she saw she had been fairly caught. 'All right, then, if you must. I expect you're going to bother me about that silly business last night.'

'That silly—' exclaimed Freddy. 'Do you call skipping about with a corpse in a toy cart a silly business? I'm living in fear of my life. Why, if the police catch me, who knows what they'll accuse me of? Aiding and abetting in a murder? Kidnapping? Or will they settle for a lesser charge of dangerous driving with an overloaded vehicle, do you suppose?'

'Shh!' said Cynthia, glancing about. 'Not so loud! Don't be ridiculous. Nobody need know about it except ourselves, as long as you keep quiet.'

'Except that the police are already investigating,' said Freddy. 'Ticky's doctor saw at once that he'd been moved after he died, and it's only a matter of time before they find out who did it.'

Cynthia put her hand to her mouth.

'Oh, goodness!' she said. 'Are you sure? Is that why the police were called? I had no idea.'

'Of course that's why the police were called. Why did you think it was?'

'Why, I don't know,' she said vaguely. 'I can't say I'd given it much thought.'

Freddy suppressed the urge to give his mother a good shake.

'Look,' he said. 'You can't wriggle out of this one. I don't know what you were thinking of, but it's perfectly clear we've made things ten times worse by doing what we did. If you'd called a doctor straightaway, then everything would have been so much easier. They'd probably have put it down to a heart attack and nobody would have been any the wiser. Now they're suspicious, and as soon as they find out where he was last night they'll be sniffing around, asking awkward questions, and then what shall you say? You'll have to admit everything.'

'*I*? What have I to admit? You're the one who did it,' said Cynthia sweetly. 'I shall tell them I had nothing to do with it.'

'You wouldn't!' he said, aghast.

'Just watch me.'

As Freddy spluttered with indignation, she put her hand on his arm.

'Look, darling,' she said persuasively. 'I expect you're right—I probably ought to have called a doctor, but the thing's done now, and if we don't want to get into trouble, it's in both our interests to say nothing. Even if they suspect, they can't prove it, and it's not as though either of *us* killed him, is it?'

'I don't know,' said Freddy. '*Did* you kill him?'

'Of course I didn't kill him! What a dreadful thing to suggest of your own mother! Freddy, I'm quite shocked at you.'

'I wouldn't put it past you.'

'Well, I didn't. It all happened exactly as I told you. He didn't feel well in the taxi, and then he collapsed outside our house and I—well, I suppose I panicked at the mention of poison.'

'All right, then, but if you didn't kill him, then who did? And why? Who wanted him dead?'

'Oh, we all wanted him dead, darling,' she said without thinking.

'What?'

'Nothing,' she said hurriedly. 'I was just joking.'

'No you weren't. What do you mean, you all wanted him dead? I thought you were all terrific pals.'

'Well, dead is a strong word,' she said. 'I mean, that's probably a *little* bit of an exaggeration, but he wasn't the nicest sort, and he did take advantage rather, and I really didn't have the cash to spare quite often, but he was always very firm and wouldn't let me off. And I expect if he was doing it with me then he was doing it with everybody—not that anyone's confessed to it in so many words, naturally, since it's not the sort of thing one talks about, but I have heard some *strong* hints—so I suppose it's always possible that he pushed things a little too far with someone. Perhaps he caught them on a bad day, or—I don't know—perhaps they couldn't afford it that week, or something. You know how one can put up with things for a while, then suddenly get sick and tired of it all, and decide that enough's enough. So if he really didn't die of a heart attack, then I expect that's what happened. Do you see?'

'No,' said Freddy, although he was beginning to have a sinking feeling. 'Why were you paying him money?'

Cynthia looked away and said nothing.

'Mother,' said Freddy, as the truth dawned. 'Do you mean to say Ticky was blackmailing you?'

CHAPTER SEVEN

'WELL—' BEGAN CYNTHIA, and shifted uncomfortably.

'How much did you pay him?' said Freddy.

'I don't know. A few hundred, perhaps? A couple of thousand. I didn't count it.'

'A *couple of thousand*? And you didn't count it?'

'How could I? I didn't pay it all in one go, and it's not as though he sent me a bill. I just paid him what I could, whenever he asked for it. Forty pounds here, fifty pounds there.'

'But how often?'

'Once a month, perhaps? A little more often? I don't know. Whenever I saw him, I suppose. Of course, I tried to avoid him but it was very difficult, since he was invited to absolutely everything, and it was either pay up or never go out at all.'

'When did it start?'

'A couple of years ago, I think. Or was it three? No, definitely two, because I'm sure it was in the autumn after we moved down to Richmond. Or was that the spring? I can't remember.

And would you please stop looking at me like that, darling? I'm trying my best to tell you what I know.'

Freddy's face was indeed a picture. As a rule, he regarded his mother with a sort of fond exasperation, but the news that she had presumably done something that had laid her open to blackmail had completely thrown him. He hesitated, but his curiosity was too strong for him.

'I shall no doubt regret asking this, but what exactly did he have on you?' he said.

Cynthia sighed crossly and drummed her fingers on the banister.

'This is very vexing,' she said. 'If I tell you then I've paid him all that money for nothing.'

'As an insurance policy it certainly seems to have failed in its purpose,' agreed Freddy dryly. 'Come on—out with it.'

'You must promise not to tell your father.'

'I won't promise anything of the kind. It's not an affair or something, is it? I'm sure he'll understand if you approach him in the right way and beg forgiveness.'

'An affair? What do you take me for?' said Cynthia indignantly. 'I should hope I'm not one of *those* women. No, it's nothing like that. Just a little matter of money, I'm afraid.'

'Ah, now we come to it,' said Freddy. 'It's not the Chemmy again, is it? I thought you'd given that up.'

'Well, I did stop for a while, after your father put his foot down,' said Cynthia. 'But once we were back on an even keel again, I didn't think there was any harm in just a *little* game among friends. Just for fun, you know. But one thing led to another, and—well—'

'You couldn't stop,' said Freddy.

'Can you blame me? I was winning at first—had quite a lucky streak, as a matter of fact, and then I started to think that perhaps I could keep going and even bring in a little extra on top of the *Clarion* stuff. After all, your father couldn't possibly object to my starting again if I was always ahead. But then I had a bad night, and then another, and I started putting down more to try and get it back, and things got worse and worse. And then Ticky started coming to the games and kept playing banker, and every time I went bank against him I lost. I've wondered since whether he mightn't have been cheating—you know, with cards up his sleeve, or something—but I have no proof of that. Then on this particular night we'd all had rather a lot to drink, I'm afraid, and things got a little out of hand, and Ticky put down the most enormous amount of money, and we all threw down even more, and he increased the bank to match *that*, and I was the one to play, and I completely lost my head and asked for another card on six even when everybody shouted at me not to, as I was convinced the next one would be a three.'

'Let me guess. It was a four.'

'How clever of you, darling. Yes, it was. Anyway, of course I lost, and to make things worse I didn't actually have the money as I'd been playing on credit. And everyone was so horrid to me for losing everything that I felt I ought to pay them back, but I couldn't. And then Ticky took me to one side and said not to worry, that he'd lend me the money, and that I could pay him back whenever I liked, and I was *so* relieved, and rather stupidly told him how glad I was that your father would never have to find out about it. It wasn't until I next saw him that I discovered he was expecting me to pay interest on the loan.'

'Is that what he called it?' said Freddy.

'Yes. Naturally, I was taken aback, as I'd scraped together the whole sum to pay him back that day, but I couldn't very well argue, so I asked him how much he wanted on top of the original amount, and he said he didn't know the exact total, but that we'd start at forty pounds for now.'

'But how much was the original amount?'

'Three hundred pounds, give or take a few guineas. I thought forty pounds would be enough interest for a loan between friends, and I said so, but it was obvious he didn't agree, and then when I complained—jokingly, you know—he just gave that awful oily smile of his and said I'd better get used to the idea of giving him money if I didn't want Herbert to know what I'd been getting up to. And that's where it all started.'

'And never ended, by the sound of it,' said Freddy. 'But why didn't you just tell Father in the first place? Surely that would have been better than letting this fellow bleed you dry for two years?'

'Well, yes, I expect it would,' said Cynthia. 'But he'd been awfully grumpy about my earlier losses, and I'd promised to keep off the cards, so I didn't want another row. And at first, you know, I didn't quite understand that I *was* being black-mailed. After all, Ticky was a friend of sorts, and friends don't do that to one another, do they?'

'Not as a rule,' said Freddy. 'But how could you bear to keep on seeing him in company once you'd realized what was hap-pening? You pretended you liked him.'

'We *all* pretended we liked him, darling,' said Cynthia. 'We had no choice—at least, I expect that's the case. I'm almost certain he'd got at Nancy, too, from something she said, and I can't think of a single reason Lady Bendish or Captain Atherton would agree to come to an evening like the one we had last night, when it's not usually their sort of thing at all. I shouldn't be a bit surprised if everybody in the party was paying him money under duress. And we all clubbed together to buy him that flask, and simply *fawned* over him for the whole evening,' she said in sudden disgust. 'Do you know, I can't think what got into me.'

'I wonder what he had on all the others,' said Freddy.

'Who knows?' said Cynthia. 'I can't imagine Sarah Bendish ever being anything less than perfectly well-behaved, but I suppose even she must have some hidden sins about which we know nothing.'

'This is all bad news for you, you know,' said Freddy. 'The police are sniffing around, thanks to us. What will happen if they discover what Ticky was up to? Even if they never find out about what we did, you were still the last one to see him alive—as they'll soon know once they've found the taxi-driver who brought you home—and you had the most thundering motive to kill him.'

'Oh, but I've been thinking about that. There's no reason for them to find out about it at all. You see, there was nothing written down. It's not as though he sent me letters or bills or anything. There's no record.'

'Can you be sure of that? Perhaps he kept a tally in a note-book. If he really was living off all his friends, then he must have kept some sort of account of things, don't you think? I mean to say, if one's going into the blackmail business, then presumably one has to keep evidence of one's victims' sins somewhere. I shouldn't be a bit surprised if he has a whole folder full of names, dates and payments tucked away in a drawer in his house.'

'Oh, goodness!' exclaimed Cynthia. 'Then what shall I do? How can we get it back? If the police find it then they'll tell your father and I'll be in the most awful trouble. Freddy, you must go and get it.'

'Now, just a minute,' said Freddy, who saw with alarm that he was about to be dragged further into the business. 'I've already transported the man's corpse to a more convenient location for you, at great risk to myself, and now you're asking me to go and burgle his house.'

'I'm not asking you to burgle anyone's house,' said Cynthia. 'All you need to do is talk your way in past that manservant of his. You're so good at that sort of thing that I'm sure you'll manage it with no difficulty at all.'

'Did this manservant know what Ticky was up to?'

'Why, I don't know. I suppose he must have.'

'Then he's hardly going to let me in, is he? I mean to say, he'll be watching for angry customers skulking about, looking for an excuse to knock on the door. What's his name?'

'Who? The manservant? How should I know, darling? All I know is that he used to creep up on one and give one a fright whenever one visited. A sneaking sort, I should say.'

'Two of a kind, it sounds like,' said Freddy thoughtfully. 'I wonder if he was in on it. The blackmail, I mean. I can't believe

Ticky did *all* the dirty work himself. Someone had to rifle through pockets and drawers for evidence of other people's naughtiness. But of course, this is all speculation, since you say you don't know whether Ticky was blackmailing anybody else.'

'But I don't care about anybody else,' said Cynthia. 'I just want to be sure he hasn't kept any record that he was blackmailing *me*. It would be too bad if it all came out in the open after I've managed to keep it a secret from your father all this time.'

'It's not Father you ought to be thinking of. All you'll get from him is a wigging. But the law has a nasty habit of hanging people who poison their acquaintances, so it's the police you need to worry about.'

'Oh dear,' said Cynthia. 'I don't want to be arrested. You must help me, Freddy. You must search the place for me, and bring back whatever it was Ticky was keeping, so I can burn it. Weaver!' she exclaimed suddenly. 'That's his name; I've just remembered. A horrid, damp little man. Go and talk to Weaver. Tell him something—anything you like, just so long as you get into the house.'

Freddy sighed. This was all starting to look inevitable. If he did not do as his mother said, and Ticky *did* have something in writing, then the police were bound to start looking at Cynthia with interest, since they would certainly track down the taxi-driver and find out that she had been the last to see Ticky alive. And after that they would no doubt start asking questions about where exactly he had died, and how he had come to be found outside number 25, Caroline Terrace, since Cynthia could not possibly have moved him herself. Freddy suddenly remembered that he had left the toy cart downstairs in the entrance-hall at Eaton Terrace, and hoped Mrs. Hanbury had put it back in the attic. There was a very real danger that the police would find out sooner or later the part he had played in the affair, and he was already in enough trouble with Mr. Bickerstaffe as it was. Freddy had not read his contract of employment lately, but he was reasonably sure it included a clause prohibiting employees of the *Clarion* from engaging in illegal activity of any kind, on pain of instant dismissal.

'Oh, very well,' he said grumpily at last. 'I'll see what I can do. It's just a pity you didn't think to pick his pocket after he died. You might have got his door key, at least, and saved me some bother.'

'Pick his pocket, indeed! What sort of person do you think I am? A common thief?' said Cynthia with a nervous laugh. 'But you'll do it, darling? Splendid. Just make sure nobody catches you. Now, I must just go and say goodbye to Mrs. Belcher and then I think I shall go home and have a little rest. I had to get up early this morning to write my column, and I do believe I'm rather tired after all the excitement of last night. You'll let me know when you've managed it, won't you? And don't tell your father!'

And with that she hurried off back up the stairs, smiling gaily as though the conversation had never taken place and she was not in danger of being arrested on suspicion of having committed at least two crimes. Freddy stood on the stairs for a minute or two, wondering what he had let himself in for, then followed her slowly back into the salon. There he spent an hour or so adroitly dodging all attempts to persuade him to embrace the temperance cause and become a benefactor of the Young Women's Abstinence Association, after which he was quite exhausted, and made up his mind to go home. He wanted to say goodbye to Amelia Drinkwater, but she was not in sight, and he glanced into a side-room, with some idea that she might be there. Instead, he saw the young woman who had earlier been showing interest in the silver, peering into a cupboard. She jumped when she saw him and gave him a fierce glare from under her heavy eyebrows.

'You'd better come out of there,' said Freddy. 'You're spoiling the look of the thing.'

'Stuck-up old cats,' she said furiously. 'Think they're it, don't they? They crowd around and stare at us, as if we were animals in a zoo. They think it's all so simple. It's all "do what we say, because we know better than you." And they give us the chipped china because we're not good enough for the best— oh no! Well, they're all stupid, and I won't be told what to do.'

'That's clear enough,' said Freddy. 'But in that case, why are you here?'

'To see things from the inside,' she said. 'You lot won't always have it this easy. Everything's going to change, and soon—you mark my words. It's about time the wealth was shared about more equally between the rich and the poor.'

'Ah,' said Freddy. 'You're here on behalf of your own cause, I see. I have a friend who believes in all that stuff, too. Beastly dull, I call it. Still, I'm all for letting people occupy themselves in whatever manner they see fit. I suppose if I made a donation towards the revolution you wouldn't go and spend it on drink?'

'Not I,' she said, accepting the proffered coin. 'Can't stand the stuff.'

'But you'd better put the teaspoons back before you go.'

She hesitated, then dug in a pocket and brought out three spoons and a pair of silver tongs, which she handed to him.

'You don't really give a hoot about politics, do you?' said Freddy.

'God helps those who help themselves,' she said. 'And I like to help myself.'

And with that she flashed him a mischievous smile that quite transformed her face, and left.

Chapter Eight

T HEN IT WAS murder?' said Inspector Entwistle.
Dr. Ingleby pursed his lips.

'I shouldn't like to commit myself in court at this stage,' he said, 'but all the signs are that he was poisoned—although with what I can't tell you yet. It wasn't cyanide, at any rate. And it wasn't strychnine either, although I suspect it was *some* sort of fast-acting alkaloid. I shall need to do more tests before I can be sure. He was certainly moved after he died, however—there's no doubt at all about that.'

'That's suspicious in itself,' said Entwistle. 'Presumably it means someone was not only with him when he died, but also had a hand in it. If they didn't, then why didn't they simply call a doctor when he collapsed, instead of going to all the trouble of moving him? No, whoever moved him killed him all right. But in that case, why did they put him outside number 25, instead of his own house?'

'I've no idea,' said Ingleby cheerfully. 'That's your job, and quite frankly I don't envy you it.' He rose. 'Very well, I must get back, but I thought you'd like to know my preliminary findings. I shall be doing some more tests this afternoon and I hope to have something for you by tomorrow.'

And with that he gave a nod and hurried out.

'What do you think, sir?' said Sergeant Bird to Entwistle.

'I think it's all distinctly fishy,' replied the inspector. 'We'd better speak to this Weaver fellow again, and find out more about what his employer had been getting up to before he died.'

'No use in doing that this morning, sir. He sent in a message to say he was going to Dorking for the weekend. He won't be back until late this afternoon, he said.'

'What? That's rather convenient for him. On Friday he was too upset to talk to us, and now he's off gallivanting around the country.'

'He's gone to visit his frail old mother, like a good boy,' said Bird.

'Hmph,' said Entwistle. 'I suppose he'll have to wait until later, then. Still, at least he wasn't too distraught to tell us where Maltravers had been that night. All right; let's go and question the waiters at this place in Piccadilly.'

The manager of Babcock's was shocked and desolated to hear the news of Ticky's tragic fate, for Mr. Maltravers had been one of his best and most generous customers. Mindful that it would not do to have people thinking that his clients were in the habit of dropping dead after dining at his establishment, he expressed himself eager to help the police in any way he could. The party had been a lively one, he said, but it had been a busy night so he had had little time to attend to them. However, he would summon Antoine, the maître d'hotel, who would no doubt have more to say. Antoine was equally shocked, and not a little worried that he was about to be blamed for the death in some way, and so was only too willing to tell what he knew. The menu was consulted and various under-waiters brought forth, and at length it was established to everyone's satisfaction that if a noxious substance had indeed been introduced to Ticky's dinner (and please God it had not), then it had certainly not originated in the kitchen, for all the food presented that evening had been served to the whole party from shared dishes—so one person alone could not have been taken ill. Would it have been possible for someone to poison Ticky's food after it had been served, Inspector Entwistle wanted to know? As to that, said Antoine, he did not know. Mr. Maltravers had been seated between Mrs. Pilkington-Soames and Mrs. Van Leeuwen, but he did not like to think that either of them might have been responsible for such a heinous act. At the mention of Cynthia's name, Sergeant Bird's ears pricked up, and he frowned but said nothing. Inspector Entwistle then wanted to know what the party had had to drink, and did his best not to whistle at the lengthy list of wines consumed.

'And they all partook of the same drinks, you say?' he said.

Antoine could not say for certain, but he *could* say that wine from each bottle had been poured into at least two or three different glasses and, he could only assume, had therefore been drunk by two or three different people. Coffee had been ordered, but, again, had been served from one pot.

'Then it sounds as though it wasn't in his drink, either,' said Entwistle. 'If everyone shared all the wines then he wouldn't have been the only one to fall ill—unless, of course, one of the ladies sitting next to him put something in his glass. We shall have to ask the members of the party, just to be sure. Did he take a digestive after dinner?'

'There was a rare Cusenier,' said Antoine. 'He was the only one of the party to drink it, but I know it was not poisoned, because he was so kind as to give me the rest of the bottle, that it might be shared among all the waiters. We all had some and it was *magnifique—sans pareil.* It was most certainly not poisoned.'

'Hmm,' said Entwistle. 'That's rather a facer, then. Perhaps he didn't take the stuff here after all.'

'I should be most relieved to hear that,' said Antoine. 'As you say, I do not see how the poison could have been introduced into anything that was consumed that night. Unless, of course, it was in the flask,' he added.

'Which flask?' said Entwistle, suddenly alert.

'Why, the little silver flask they gave him. I believe it was a birthday present or something of the kind. It was engraved with his name. He poured some of the Cognac into it, and I was forced to turn my face away.' He lowered his voice. 'Mr. Maltravers was a good customer, of course, but it was a scandal what he did there, and I did not wish him to see my thoughts.'

'Do you think someone put poison in the flask?' said the inspector.

Antoine shrugged.

'I do not know,' he said. 'But any one of them might have done it when they passed it around the table to examine it and exclaim over it.'

Entwistle and Bird glanced at one another.

'Are you quite sure that is what they did?' said Entwistle.

'Quite sure,' said Antoine.

'You say he unwrapped the present, then put the Cognac in it, and then passed it around the table?'

'*Non*, first was the passing-around, then was the Cognac. Gaston, this is what happened, *hein*?'

'*Oui, monsieur*,' said the young waiter thus addressed, who had been standing nearby in case he was wanted. 'The ladies screamed with much delight at the flask, although the gentlemen were a little more reserved.'

'I don't suppose you saw anybody put something in it, did you?' said the inspector, looking from Antoine to Gaston, then, as they both shook their heads, went on, 'I mean to say, it might not have been obvious that they were doing it. It might have looked as though they were examining it closely, or feeling the quality of it.'

'I saw nothing of the kind,' said Gaston.

'Nor did I,' said Antoine. 'Or, shall we say, they *all* looked at it closely, and so for that matter it might have been any of them.'

'He didn't happen to leave the flask here when he left, did he?' said Sergeant Bird.

Both men shook their heads, and Entwistle and Bird glanced at one another again.

'It's all looking very suspicious,' said the former as they left Babcock's half an hour later. 'Not least because we now seem to have a missing silver flask. There was certainly nothing of the sort in the dead man's pockets.'

'No,' said Bird. 'I wonder what happened to it.'

'Well, this Antoine was sure he had it with him when he left. I wonder whether the murderer took it. If that's how the poison was administered then that would explain why it wasn't found on him.'

'Might it have dropped out of his pocket?'

'It might have,' said Entwistle, 'but not in Caroline Terrace, or we'd have found it. But the restaurant seem to think he took a cab home, so it's possible he dropped it there. We'll have to track the driver down.' He took out his notebook and consulted it as they walked. 'Let's have a look at this list of names. Who have we got here? Denis and Nancy Beasley. Captain Maurice Atherton—is that the famous explorer, do you think? Lady Bendish, Blanche Van Leeuwen, Cynthia Pilkington-Soames. We'll have to speak to them all—and especially those last two, since they were apparently sitting next to him. Perhaps we ought to wait until Ingleby has more to tell us about what killed him.'

Sergeant Bird was frowning again.

'Pilkington-Soames was the name of that young reporter,' he said. 'He said he was a friend of Maltravers. I wonder if it's any relation.'

'It sounds like it,' said Inspector Entwistle with sudden interest. 'Why was he nosing around? Is he really press?'

'He had a card from the *Clarion*, and it looked real enough to me. I wonder whether he knows anything. He was trying to get information out of me the other day.'

'Was he, indeed? Did you tell him anything?'

'I didn't have much to tell,' said the sergeant. 'We didn't know anything ourselves on Friday. But he did hint that he had an "in" on that sort of society, and that he was willing to try and find out what he could about what happened.'

'Presumably in exchange for an "in" on what we're doing, yes? Well, I don't much like the sound of that. Better keep him at arm's length.'

'I expect you're right, sir,' said Bird, 'but I shouldn't say no to anything he might care to tell us, if he really can find out information that we can't. And there's the name, too. If he is related to one of the suspects it might be better to allow him to think we're helping him. That way he might let something slip.'

'Well, just as long as you don't give him anything confidential from our side,' said Entwistle. 'We don't want him jumping to half-baked conclusions and printing them in that paper of his. The press are more a hindrance than a help at the best of times, and the last thing we need now is to have this fellow wandering about, getting in the way and making the case more complicated than it already is.'

'Don't worry, I'll be careful,' promised the sergeant.

CHAPTER NINE

TRUE TO HIS promise, Freddy visited number 24, Caroline Terrace several times on Saturday and Sunday in an attempt to catch Ticky's servant, Weaver, at home, but it seemed the man had gone away for the weekend, for there was no answer to his knock. By his seventh unsuccessful attempt on Sunday evening, Freddy was beginning to contemplate whether it might not be possible to get in through a window and search the place, but swiftly brought himself up short. He had already been drawn further into the affair than he liked, and he had no wish to add breaking and entering to the list of offences that might be held against him if the police ever found out the part he had played in Ticky's last journey. No; his mother had got herself into this scrape, and while he was willing to help her as far as he could, he drew the line at risking a spell in prison. He would wait until Weaver returned, and get into the house through the front door.

On Monday he was wanted at the paper, and so had no opportunity to visit Caroline Terrace until late in the afternoon, but when he eventually arrived he found to his dismay that the police had got there before him, for there was a stolid-looking constable standing outside the front door, writing in a notebook. Freddy's first thought was that they had found out Ticky's secret and had come to search the house, but the policeman soon informed him otherwise.

'Burglary,' he said briefly, when Freddy had introduced himself and his newspaper. 'Man went away for the weekend and got back to find that the house had been broken into.'

'Anything stolen?' said Freddy, feeling in his pocket for a pencil—although his mind was not strictly on the story, for it was mainly occupied in wondering which of Ticky's victims had got there before him.

'Doesn't look like it. Odd, as there's some valuable stuff in the house. The man who owns the place died a few days ago, and his manservant was away, so it may be that someone had been watching the house, looking for an opportunity to get in when it was empty.'

'I can't see any broken windows,' said Freddy, looking up at the house. 'I take it they got in through the back?'

'That's right,' agreed the constable. 'There's a mews of sorts on Bourne Street. It looks like they went in that way and over the back wall.'

'One thief? More than one?'

'Just the one, it looks like.'

'I wonder why he didn't take anything,' said Freddy.

'Beats me,' said the constable. 'Perhaps he was disturbed before he had the chance, although he was there long enough, to judge by the state of the place. There are drawers overturned everywhere and papers scattered all over the floor. I guess he was looking for something in particular.'

'I see,' said Freddy thoughtfully. 'Do you think he found it?'

'Not according to the manservant,' said the other. 'He wasn't happy at the mess, but he couldn't see anything missing. He's just having another look now.' Here he stopped and looked Freddy up and down. 'I must say, you press chaps sniff things out pretty quickly. How did you know to come here?'

'I didn't, really,' said Freddy. 'I was here about another case. The man who died last week. I understand there were suspicious circumstances, and I was just passing on the off-chance that I might find Inspector Entwistle here.'

'He's supposed to be on his way,' said the policeman. 'But he's a busy man, so who knows when he'll arrive?'

'Is Weaver in the house now?' said Freddy. 'Would you mind awfully if I knocked? He might be able to give me something for the paper.'

'We-ell, I'm not sure about that,' said the constable doubtfully. 'I don't know whether that's allowed—'

He was interrupted just then by the sound of the front door opening behind him. A man came out and said:

'I have had another look around, constable, and I cannot see anything missing. I think we must assume that the burglar was frightened off by something, since Mr. Maltravers had many valuable articles in his possession which one would expect to have been of great interest to a thief.'

Freddy examined this newcomer with interest. Weaver was of middle height, with slick, black hair and a face that was almost ghostly white. In appearance he was not unlike Ticky Maltravers himself, albeit some years younger. Although there was nothing strictly offensive in his appearance—for he was perfectly clean and tidy—there was something nonetheless repellent about him. Whether it were his unsmiling manner, or his reluctance to meet one's eye, could not be told, but if any man could have been said to look like a blackmailer's manservant, then Weaver was that man. Freddy now seized his chance.

'Hallo,' he said. 'Mr. Weaver, isn't it? I'm from the *Clarion.*' Here he waved his card, but carefully kept his thumb over the surname in case Weaver recognized it. 'I understand your employer died suddenly a few days ago, and I hear you were quite his right-hand man. They tell me he never stirred without you, and relied wholly upon your counsel. I don't suppose you'd care to say a few words to our readers about the terrible tragedy? I know Mr. Maltravers was well known in high circles, but I think it only fair that everyone know that his fame and success weren't *all* his own work, and that the value of a loyal servant simply can't be over-estimated.'

Weaver's expression did not change during this speech, and it was impossible to say whether he believed a word of it. He was clearly very wary.

'What is it you wish to know?' he said.

'Suppose we go inside,' suggested Freddy. 'It's coldish out here, and not exactly conducive to talking about personal matters, what with the police crawling all over the place—if you'll excuse my saying so,' he added over his shoulder to the constable.

Weaver hesitated for a moment.

'Very well,' he said. 'But I believe we must remain in the hall, as the rest of the house is at present unfit for occupation following this most unfortunate burglary.'

'Ah, yes,' said Freddy, following him into the house. 'Despicable behaviour, what? I mean to say, taking advantage of someone's death to rob his house. It's hardly the mark of an honourable man, is it? Not that theft is an honourable profession, of course, but one might have supposed them to have *some* level below which they will not stoop.'

'Alas, it seems not,' said Weaver. He paused outside the door to the sitting-room and pushed it open. 'As you can see, the burglar went through the house very thoroughly.'

Freddy peered in and saw that he was right: the whole room had been turned upside-down. Tables had been upended and cushions dragged off chairs, while a whole bookshelf had been emptied onto the floor, and a tall lamp stood tipped half over by the window, its shade comically askew. Even the rug had been rolled up. Whatever the thief had been looking for, he had obviously searched with a fine-tooth comb.

'Good Lord!' exclaimed Freddy. 'That's going to take some time to clear up. This burglar of yours is rather destructive, I see. I expect things wouldn't seem half so bad if he'd left the place tidy. But nothing was taken, you say?'

'I do not think so.'

'That's a queer thing, don't you think? Why go to all the bother, if not to help oneself to the silver? I don't suppose the Burglars' Association will be giving this chap a merit card.'

'The thief was not looking for ordinary valuables,' said Weaver.

'No? Then what was he looking for?'

The man did not reply immediately, but the corners of his mouth turned up briefly in a complacent smile. It did not suit him and the effect was somewhat alarming. Then he fixed Freddy with a cold, insolent stare, and said:

'Whatever it was, he did not find it, because it is not here. Nobody who comes will ever find it, so you may tell them they needn't bother.'

'I don't quite understand,' said Freddy, taken aback.

'Oh, there's no need to pretend. You may not know me, but I know perfectly well who you are, Mr. Pilkington-Soames. I make it my business to know people. Mr. Maltravers found me a most satisfactory servant in that respect.'

'I'm sure he did,' said Freddy. 'And I expect he left you well provided for, eh?'

'That is so,' said Weaver with a bow. '*Very* well provided for, as a matter of fact.' Again there was the unpleasant smile. 'You may tell your mother that I shall be most happy to see her here on the first of next month. Mr. Maltravers was somewhat irregular in his habits, but I propose to make it a regular thing. I find it easier to keep accounts that way.'

'Ah,' said Freddy. There was no doubt at all that the interview was going very badly. Not only had he not succeeded in finding the evidence of blackmail, it was also now abundantly clear that Ticky's death had not brought it to a halt, but had merely caused responsibility for it to pass to someone else.

That being the case, there seemed little point in continuing the conversation.

'Very well, then,' he said. 'I shall—er—tell my mother what you said.'

'Do,' said Weaver. 'You might also mention that I am not as foolish as my employer was. He made the mistake of trusting his friends, and died for it—oh yes, I am quite certain that is what happened. I dare say we shall never find out who did it, since naturally nobody will want the police to look into the matter *too* closely—after all, who knows what uncomfortable truths might emerge? But I have the advantage of him in that respect, as I am of lowly status, and nobody will invite *me* to dinner for my birthday. You are not the first to come knocking. I have had one or two visitors already today, but I sent them away. Let it be understood that I trust nobody.'

'I should say that was very wise, in your line of work,' said Freddy, and Weaver smirked.

'Until next time,' he said with another bow.

Freddy went out and took a deep breath of fresh air.

'The Tick and the Weevil,' he said to himself. 'What a loathsome pair they make!'

'I beg your pardon, sir?' said the policeman.

'Nothing, nothing,' said Freddy. 'I don't think this will make much of a story after all, constable. Weaver had nothing to tell me that I didn't already know. I think I shall have to look elsewhere.'

He set off down Caroline Terrace, wanting nothing more than to brush the dust of number 24 off his feet, for he felt almost grubby after his encounter with Weaver. But what was he to do now? His mother had sent him to try and find evidence that Ticky had been blackmailing her, but Weaver had as good as told him that it was not in the house. Then where was it? And how could Weaver be stopped, if indeed he really did intend to continue where his former employer had left off? And, of course, there was the minor question of how Ticky had died. Had he really been poisoned? It was looking increasingly likely.

His last question was very soon answered when a motor-car drew up, and Inspector Entwistle and Sergeant Bird got out.

'Good afternoon, gentlemen,' said Freddy as they met. 'I'm afraid you've missed the burglary. The chap went off hours ago and didn't stay for an encore.'

'You're a sharp one,' said Entwistle. 'I hope you're not going to get under our feet again.'

'No, no,' said Freddy. 'Just doing an honest day's work, as always. Do you have any news on the Maltravers case?'

'You talk to him, Bird,' said the inspector. 'And remember what I said.'

He went off. Freddy watched him go.

'What did he mean by that?' he said. 'What *did* he say?'

'He told me never to trust the press,' said the sergeant.

'I say, that's rather unkind. Still, you won't listen to him, will you? I don't suppose you've found out what killed Ticky?'

'Looks like it was poison,' said Bird. 'With any luck, we'll know exactly which one by tomorrow.'

'Dear me,' said Freddy in some trepidation. 'Do you have anyone in particular in mind?'

'Why, I don't know. It appears the gentleman had spent the evening with some of his friends at Babcock's, which is by way of being a fashionable restaurant among your lot.'

'Yes, I know the place,' said Freddy.

'We don't know exactly how the poison got into him, but it's more than likely it was given to him over dinner.'

'You mean by one of his friends?' said Freddy.

'Exactly,' said Bird. 'Perhaps by the person sitting next to him. As it happens, Mr. Maltravers was sitting next to a Mrs. Cynthia Pilkington-Soames. That's your name, isn't it, sir? Any relation?'

'My mother,' said Freddy promptly, since he had been expecting the question sooner or later. 'Yes, I've spoken to her, and she mentioned something of the sort. She was terribly upset. Rather unfortunate, what? I had no idea she was one of the party when I saw you the other day. I expect your ears pricked up when you heard the name.'

'You might say that,' said Bird.

'If you're going to ask me whether she killed him, I shall tell you frankly that I have no idea, although I doubt it very much,' said Freddy. 'She's quite ridiculous most of the time, but I'm fond of the old girl, and I can say pretty much for certain that she's not generally in the habit of murdering people. At least, if she is, she's never been caught at it yet.'

'I see,' said Bird.

'Have you talked to her?' said Freddy.

'Not yet,' said the sergeant cautiously. 'The investigation is still in the early stages, but I dare say we'll speak to her soon.'

'Of course, it's going to be dashed unpleasant for her, to have the police sniffing around the place. Her heart's not strong, you see, and she's terribly frail. Quite the little mouse, in fact. Are you going to be gentle with her? I mean, you don't intend to drag her to the station in handcuffs and knock her about, or anything?'

'Certainly not,' said the sergeant.

Freddy resisted the temptation to say, 'That's a pity,' and went on:

'Do you remember what we said last week, sergeant? I promised to try and find out what I could, in return for information for my modest little news pieces. I don't suppose you can tell me anything now?'

'Aren't you supposed to tell me something first, sir?' said Bird.

'I would if I knew anything, but Mother has been sobbing all weekend and I haven't been able to get a word out of her. She's distraught about Ticky's death—simply devastated. I expect they all are, in fact. Terrible end to a birthday party, what?'

'Ah, yes,' said Bird. 'I understand they gave him a silver flask as a present. I don't suppose you saw it yourself, did you?'

'No, I didn't. One of those affairs to keep whisky in for medicinal purposes, do you mean?'

'It was brandy in this case,' said the sergeant. 'I wondered whether your mother might have mentioned to you what became of it.'

'No. Why? Is it missing?' said Freddy.

'Not exactly. Or, at least, we've barely begun searching yet, so I expect it'll turn up soon,' said the sergeant vaguely, for he did not want Freddy to think it important.

'Perhaps he left it at Babcock's,' said Freddy, although he was certain this was not the case. The most awful foreboding was stealing over him. 'Listen, I must go. I shall tell you anything I find out, but in the meantime I expect there'll be an inquest, what?'

'I dare say,' said Bird.

Freddy bade him goodbye and hurried off, frowning. What had his mother said on Friday? Yes: he was sure she had mentioned that Ticky was drinking from a flask in the taxi on the way home, but the police had presumably not found it on his body, since they were looking for it. Did that mean they believed it had contained the poison? And where was the flask now? Freddy had a dreadful suspicion that his mother knew exactly where it was—nay, that she had herself abstracted it from Ticky's pocket—and had purposely kept it from him. He had no idea where she was now, but he would have to speak to her again as soon as possible, since it rather looked as though she had complicated matters even further.

'Drat the woman!' he said to himself. 'Why must she go and get herself into this sort of fix? And why must *I* be the one to get her out of it? And now there's this Weaver fellow, who's as good as told me to spread the word that business is continuing as usual. What have I to do with it? I've kept my nose clean—well, more or less—so I don't see why I should have to get mixed up with blackmailers. I shall find Mother and give her a piece of my mind.'

And having worked himself up into a fine grump, he set off back to Fleet Street.

Chapter Ten

'NICOTINE?' SAID INSPECTOR Entwistle. 'That's a new one on me.'

'No doubt about it, though,' said Dr. Ingleby. 'There was enough in his body to have killed him twice over, had they wanted to. Very poisonous, nicotine. Just a few drops in his drink would have done it.'

'Wouldn't he have noticed the taste?'

'It depends,' said Ingleby. 'Didn't you say they'd all drunk rather a lot that evening? He'd certainly eaten more than his fair share, to judge from what was left of his stomach contents, so it's possible that his palate wasn't in any fit state to taste very much at all. And now I must run, but it's all in my report there. Let me know if there's anything you'd like explaining.'

He went out, leaving Entwistle to pore over the report at his leisure.

'Nicotine, eh?' said Sergeant Bird, who had arrived just in time to hear what the doctor had to say. 'That's easy enough to get hold of. Anyone might have a store of it at home. My old dad uses a nicotine solution on his roses. One of the party might have kept a little bottle of the stuff in his pocket, ready to put a few drops in Maltravers' drink when the opportunity presented itself. Do you think it really was in the flask, sir? And where *is* the flask?'

'Well, we've found no trace of it so far,' said Entwistle. 'Perhaps he dropped it in the taxi.'

'No, he didn't,' said Bird, remembering his news. 'That's what I was coming to tell you: Johnson's called to say he traced the driver this morning. He gave the cab a look-over, but it wasn't there.'

'Hmm,' said Entwistle. 'What did the driver say?'

The sergeant looked pleased with himself.

'Funny you should ask, sir, but it seems that Maltravers wasn't alone in that taxi.'

'Oh?'

'No. There was a woman with him. The driver didn't hear her full name, but he heard Maltravers calling her Cynthia. They got out at Eaton Terrace.'

'Mrs. Pilkington-Soames, eh?' said Entwistle. 'Any funny business going on, do you suppose?'

'Not of that sort, sir. Or at least, it doesn't look like it. The taxi-driver said Maltravers seemed unwell, and she looked as though she was trying to keep as far away from him as possible. He noticed it in particular, he said, because he has a sister who's the same way—can't stand to be near people when they're sick.'

'Did either of them say anything of interest?'

'Driver says Maltravers was very red in the face, and mentioned something about having eaten too much, so Mrs.

Pilkington-Soames suggested he take a nip from his flask, which he did. Then they got out and Maltravers said he needed some fresh air, and that's all the driver heard before he went off.'

'Then she was the last person to see him alive, by the sound of it,' said Entwistle. 'I think we shall have to have a word with this Mrs. Pilkington-Soames. The disappearing flask is very suspicious.'

'I've already tried her at home in Eaton Terrace, but no luck,' said Bird.

'No wonder that son of hers has been sniffing around. I'll bet he knows far more than he's letting on.'

'I shouldn't be surprised. Still, though, he does seem to have his uses. He's found a possible witness to the burglary at Maltravers' house.'

'Oh? Who's that?'

'No-one reliable, unfortunately. He's a tramp who goes by the name of Ugly John and spends most of his days hanging around the New Court. He swears he saw a dark-skinned man loitering suspiciously on Bourne Street early on Monday morning.'

'Did he, indeed?' said Entwistle, unconvinced. 'And I expect this Ugly John was as sober as a judge at the time, yes?'

'I think that's too much to hope for, sir,' said Bird. 'Still, it's something.'

'I doubt anything will come of it, since nothing was taken,' said Entwistle. 'Very well, then; we'd better start questioning these people who were at Babcock's. Bird, you keep on trying Mrs. Pilkington-Soames, and you'd better go and speak to Lady Bendish and Mrs. Van Leeuwen too. I'll take Mr. and Mrs. Beasley, and Captain Atherton.'

'All right, sir,' said Bird, trying to hide his disappointment, for he had been very keen to speak to the famous explorer, who was something of a hero of his.

'We'll meet back here later and compare notes,' said Entwistle, who had also followed Atherton's adventures with interest, and had no hesitation in exploiting his seniority in this manner.

Bird nodded resignedly, and went off to do his duty.

HAD THE TWO men been in a position to hear the conversation which had taken place between Captain Atherton and his manservant only the day before, they might have looked less favourably upon their hero. Atherton was sitting in his armchair at about two o'clock on Monday afternoon, reading his newspaper, when he felt a presence at his elbow.

'Well?' he said, without looking up from the shipping page. 'Did you get them?'

'Alas, no, sir,' said Mahomet. 'If they are in the house, then they are well hidden. I looked under everything and behind everything and inside everything, and there was nothing. I am convinced that they have been taken elsewhere.'

'But they were in the house once,' said Atherton. 'I know they were, because the scoundrel showed me them—waved them in front of my face, in fact. I wonder where he put them.'

'Perhaps he gave them to his man for safekeeping,' said Mahomet.

'Good Lord, I hope not. That would be the worst of all possible worlds. What if he gets ideas of his own?'

'Then we must think of some solution,' said Mahomet.

———————

LARRY BENDISH WAS not a man to stoop to burglary, but he was very worried about his mother, who had become withdrawn and silent since Friday. He was eager to do something to help her, but since she would not admit that she had any particular worries, there seemed nothing he could do even to comfort her. But he could not bear to do nothing, and so on Tuesday morning he found his steps turning in the direction of Caroline Terrace. Number 24 looked the same as any of the other houses on the street, and he stood outside it for a few minutes, staring irresolutely at the front door, as though by doing so all his problems would magically resolve themselves. At last, he approached and knocked, although he hardly knew what he would say if someone answered. To his relief, no-one did, and so he turned away, and bumped straight into Denis Beasley. They greeted one another in some embarrassment.

'Nobody's answering,' said Larry, then, feeling as though he ought to explain what he was doing there, continued, 'I—er—came with a message of condolence from my mother.'

Denis Beasley might reasonably have asked Larry who he was intending to deliver the message *to*, since Ticky was known to have no family, but he did not, and merely muttered in agreement. The two men turned away from the house and walked together back up the road.

'Has your mother heard from the police at all?' said Denis. 'I expect you know they think it's murder?'

'Yes,' replied Larry.

'Dashed awkward business, don't you think? I mean to say, presumably they suspect one of us of having done it. Naturally it was nothing to do with me, but still, it's not exactly fun having the police prying into one's private affairs.'

'No, I suppose not,' said Larry. 'My mother hasn't said much. I think she prefers not to think about that sort of thing.'

Denis let out a humourless laugh.

'I only wish I could do that,' he said. 'But I was never much good at ignoring uncomfortable truths. I should advise your mother to start looking facts in the face.'

'What do you mean?' said Larry, looking up suddenly.

'Nothing, nothing. It's been an odd few days and I suppose my thoughts have been running away with me. Here's my car. Can I offer you a lift back?'

'No thanks,' said Larry, who disliked Denis for reasons that he knew were not altogether rational. 'I prefer to walk.'

'I'll tell Ann I saw you,' said Denis, and drove off.

'I SHALL MISS you dreadfully when you leave me,' said Nancy Beasley to Ann Chadwick, who was hunting about for a stamp. 'But we'll keep your room for you here, just in case you ever need it.'

'I don't think I shall, but thank you all the same,' said Ann. She smiled her serene, competent smile, and sat down to address the envelope.

'Your Larry is such a nice boy,' went on Nancy. 'And you did it so neatly, too! Quite expertly, in fact.'

'What do you mean?' said Ann.

'Why, the way you stole him from under Amelia's nose, darling. Now, don't deny it. It was as smart a job as ever I saw. He was all set to propose to her, I'm sure of it, but then you came along and looked at him sideways and he suddenly lost interest.'

'Nonsense,' said Ann, laughingly. 'There was never anything between Larry and Amelia. She told me so herself.'

'Of course she did,' said Nancy. 'The girl has no lack of pride, I'll say that for her. She saw the game was up and made the best of it.'

Ann shook her head, serious now.

'It's not true, you know, and I should feel simply awful if it were. They've known one another since they were children, and they're good pals, that's all. As a matter of fact, I shall always be grateful to Amelia for introducing us.'

'I should have thought a girl with your brains might have made it her business to marry a richer man, but you haven't done too badly, all told,' said Nancy, and with that lost interest in the subject, as she was wont to do. She idly examined the rings on her fingers. 'I wonder when the police will call,' she said after a few moments.

'Do you think they will?'

'Oh, I should imagine so, don't you? If Ticky was poisoned, then it must have been one of us. I wonder which? Probably Cynthia, I expect. She went off in a taxi with him, so she had plenty of opportunity. I only hope she's buried the evidence somewhere.'

'Goodness!' exclaimed Ann. 'You don't really think she did it, do you?'

'Well, if she did, then she's done me the most tremendous favour. The man was a ghastly parasite, and I can't think why someone didn't do it earlier. I'd have done it myself if I'd had the nerve.'

'What do you mean? Why was he a parasite?'

'Why, he lived off us all, darling,' said Nancy carelessly. 'He found out our secrets and demanded money in return for his silence. And not only money,' she added, as Ann exclaimed. 'You don't think he was invited to everything because he was *liked*, do you?'

'I don't know,' said Ann. 'Isn't that why people usually receive invitations?'

'Not in Ticky's case. He was invited because everyone was afraid of him and what he might do if he was left out.'

'Good heavens!' said Ann. 'Was he blackmailing you too?'

'Of course he was,' said Nancy. 'I don't know why I let him do it, since it's not as though I'd done anything terrible. It's all Constance Featherstone's fault, of course. If it wasn't so beastly important to be in with her, I shouldn't have cared in the slightest, but to get in with *her* these days one also has to get in with Marjorie Belcher, and I may have done one or two things in the past that she wouldn't approve of. There was one rather unfortunate episode with the police a few years ago, after I'd had just a *little* too much to drink. Luckily they let me off with a caution, but that sort of thing tends to make one *persona non grata* when it comes to sitting on the board of trustees of a dry charity. That might not be so bad in itself, but there was also a time, a few years ago, when I dabbled a little with cocaine. Nothing serious, you understand, and I wouldn't touch the horrid stuff now, but at the time everyone was doing it so one felt one had to join in, and I'm afraid Ticky found out about that, too.'

'Did you pay him a lot of money?' said Ann. 'I mean, you're not in trouble, are you?'

'Oh, no, nothing like that. I *was* running a little short of funds last year, but then poor Father died in the October, and things were all right again. Quite all right, in fact.'

'I'm glad to hear it,' said Ann. 'Blackmail is an awful business.'

'Anyway, you'd better not mention it to the police, or they might think I did it. And don't tell Denis, either. He doesn't know about the cocaine, and I'd rather it stayed that way—besides, things have been so much better between us since I threatened to divorce him if he didn't give up that ghastly blonde with the cheap dresses, and I don't want to give him an excuse to stray again.'

'I shan't say a word,' promised Ann.

'Splendid,' said Nancy. 'Then perhaps we'll all get through this yet.'

CHAPTER ELEVEN

B Y WEDNESDAY FREDDY had spent two fruitless days trying to find his mother, to ask her whether she had taken the flask from Ticky's pocket, and he was starting to think that she was deliberately avoiding him. When he went to Eaton Terrace, he was told she had gone down to Richmond, but when he followed her there, he found only his father, who had seen her briefly the day before but had no idea where she was now, although he supposed she was off gallivanting in London as usual—and what was all this about Ticky Maltravers dropping dead?

It was hardly a surprise, of course; Cynthia had an exceptional talent for shying away from uncomfortable truths, and since Freddy knew he was by now inextricably linked in her mind with the unpleasant events of last Thursday night, he supposed it was only natural to expect that she would want to avoid him for a while. But this was more than simply an uncomfortable truth, for the police would not be fooled forever, and the memory of the ridiculous escapade she had persuaded him into was fresh in Freddy's mind. It would not do for the two of them to be arrested for a crime they had not committed—that *he* had not committed, at any rate—purely because she had panicked at the sight of a dead body.

For the present, however, there was nothing he could do except to loiter around Scotland Yard as much as he could, under the pretence of following the case for the *Clarion*. The story had got out now, and was all over the other papers, so at least he had a convincing excuse for it. To his surprise, he found that the police had already spoken to all the members of the party, including Cynthia, although Sergeant Bird would tell him little of what had been said, and seemed to have become much more wary. It was inevitable, now that it was known he was Cynthia's son, but still it was an inconvenience, for he was nervous at being kept in the dark. If only he could have been absolutely certain that his mother had *not* killed Ticky, then he would have thought nothing of jumping in himself to help the police look for the murderer, but Cynthia's behaviour since Ticky's death had been so altogether suspicious that he was afraid the trail might lead back to her in the end, and exasperated as he was at her, he did not wish to see her arrested, so he hesitated, worried at what he might discover if he started poking about. Much to his disquiet, the police had now officially announced that Ticky had died of nicotine poisoning, and that they strongly suspected the poison to have been administered by means of some Cognac in a silver flask, which was now missing. But even though Cynthia was known to have been the last person to see Ticky alive, she had not yet been arrested, although Freddy was certain it could be only a matter of time. He wished to find her—first, to find out what she had done with the flask, and second, to give her a good shake at having caused so much trouble, but still she remained stubbornly elusive, and so he was forced to suppress his annoyance and do his best to ignore the digs from his fellow-reporters at the *Clarion*, who had no compunction in teasing him mercilessly about his mother's connection with the case.

On Thursday an inquest was opened, and Freddy went along with his notebook, although he knew it was likely to be adjourned—and indeed, that proved to be the case. The police wanted more time to gather evidence, and so proceedings were swiftly brought to a close. Outside the coroner's court Freddy was patting his pockets in search of a cigarette, when he spotted someone he recognized emerging from the building. It was Amelia Drinkwater, who was looking very pretty in a pink coat and a cunning hat, and who greeted him like an old friend.

'Hallo,' he said in surprise. 'I didn't notice you in there. I shouldn't have thought this was your sort of place.'

'It isn't,' she said. 'I came here to find out what's going on, although I might as well have saved myself the trouble for all the good it was. I thought there'd be a jury, and that we'd hear all the evidence, and then perhaps I'd have an idea of what Mummy is being so mysterious about. But instead there was a lot of deadly dull legal stuff and no conclusion at all!'

'No, it's not likely we'd have heard anything exciting today,' said Freddy. 'This hearing was just a formality, really.'

Amelia pouted.

'Bother,' she said. 'I was hoping to play detective, but I shall just have to find something else to do instead.'

'Why did you want to play detective?' asked Freddy.

'Why, because I want to know who murdered Ticky, of course!' she said.

'But the police are taking care of that.'

'Nonsense,' she said. 'I don't believe they'll find out a thing. You know what our sort are like: they think they're above everyone else, and that the rules don't apply to them, and they don't want people poking their noses into their private business, thank you very much. The police won't get anything out of them, you'll see. They'll clam up and turn in on themselves, and we'll never find out what happened.'

'But don't you think that might be best?' said Freddy. 'After all, one doesn't like to think of one's friends being arrested for murder.'

'Well, you're just as bad as them if you think that,' said Amelia sternly. 'Murder's a horrid business, even if it *was* Ticky. I didn't like him, but he didn't deserve to die.'

'Perhaps not to die, no,' Freddy conceded unwillingly.

'And I don't like to think of Mummy being under suspicion for the rest of her life. She says she doesn't care, but she's been nervy and absent-minded ever since it happened, so I'm sure she doesn't mean it—and besides, I know Andrew won't exactly be thrilled at the thought of her being dragged into it. He's my stepfather, and rather stiff about that sort of thing. He's in Singapore at the moment, but I don't suppose he'll be any too pleased to find this hanging over Mummy's head when he gets back.'

'Does your mother have any idea what happened?' said Freddy.

'She didn't see a thing, she says—she was too busy being dreadfully bored. But *someone* must have given him the poison, and I'm certain it wasn't her. The police came the other day, you know, and asked her a lot of questions. They seemed very interested in a silver brandy flask that everybody bought for Ticky's birthday present.'

'Oh, yes?' said Freddy with interest. 'What did they want to know?'

'Well, they *said* it was missing, and they want to find it. Of course, they never like to give away what they're thinking, but it was pretty obvious they believe the poison was in it. I dare say Ticky dropped it on the way home, and some passing tramp found it. I say,' she said suddenly. 'If someone picked it up then they might have drunk out of it. I wonder whether anyone else has dropped dead mysteriously in London in the past few days? If they have, then I'll bet that's where the flask got to.'

'I don't think anything like that has happened,' said Freddy. 'We tend to hear about these things pretty quickly at the paper, so if someone had died suddenly like that, you can be sure we'd know about it.'

'Oh, yes, you're a reporter, aren't you?' she said, looking at him with renewed interest. 'Then you *must* want to know the truth, surely? Won't you get showered with praise if you find the culprit?'

'Well, I suppose there would be some benefit to it,' he said cautiously.

'Then that's settled,' she said. 'You shall help me. We'll solve the mystery together and present it to the police, then you'll get a promotion and I shall have my picture in the paper.'

'This is nothing to do with your mother really, is it?' said Freddy. 'You just want to have the fun of investigating a murder.'

'We-ell, yes, perhaps just a little,' she said, and she admitted it so mischievously and charmingly that he was caught. 'But that's truly not the only reason. I really am worried about Mummy—and Larry's mother too, as I'm rather fond of her. She's a sweet thing, and takes life terribly seriously. I'm sure she must be going through agonies at all these horrid pressmen slithering about outside the house—oh, how rude of me,' she said suddenly, putting a hand over her mouth. 'Of course I didn't mean you!'

'I should jolly well hope not,' said Freddy.

'Look, come and see Mummy,' she said. 'You're one of us, so I know she'll say things to you that she wouldn't tell the police.'

'But why won't she say anything to you? And why are you so sure she knows something?'

'She won't talk to me because she thinks I'm still a child,' said Amelia. 'But she must know something. I've read lots of detective-stories, and there's *always* a witness who sees something vital but doesn't realize at the time how important it is.'

'Is there?'

'Of course! And you're a reporter, so you must have had plenty of practice at putting subtle questions to people so they don't understand what's really being asked of them. I'm sure you'll think of something terribly clever to say.'

'Oh—ah,' said Freddy, whose facility for clever remarks seemed to have deserted him for the present. There was no doubting Amelia Drinkwater's enthusiasm, but she appeared to have the queerest ideas of how investigators went about their business—and it was perfectly obvious that she knew nothing of Ticky's nefarious activities, or their implications. Much as he would have liked to do as she said, that he might gaze at her all afternoon, he thought it only fair to give her a hint, at least. He did not want to be responsible for her finding out something about her mother that she would rather not have known.

'Look here, Miss—' he began.

'It's not Miss, it's Amelia, silly,' she said.

'Er—yes, and I'm Freddy.'

'I know that,' she said. 'What is it?'

'I—'

She was regarding him innocently with her wide, blue eyes. Freddy gave it up.

'Where does she live?' he said.

She positively beamed.

'Brook Street,' she said. 'If we go now, we'll just catch her at home.'

The lady in question was indeed at home, and on the telephone, to judge by the female voice that came drifting down from upstairs as they arrived. Amelia led Freddy into an expansive sitting-room with high ceilings and large windows.

'You'd better sit down,' she said, directing him to a Spartan-looking chair in the modern style, which was precisely as comfortable as might have been expected from its appearance. Then she went out to fetch her mother, while Freddy looked about him. The apartment was furnished stylishly and fashionably, and spoke of having had much money spent on it in recent times. It did not seem to fit with what he had seen of Amelia Drinkwater up to now, and he wondered who had been responsible for it. He soon found out as Amelia returned, followed by another woman with golden hair. He jumped to his feet.

'This is my mother, Blanche Van Leeuwen,' said Amelia. 'Mummy, this is Freddy Pilkington-Soames.'

'Hallo, Freddy,' purred Blanche.

Freddy took a sudden step backwards and let out a strangled exclamation which he just managed to turn into a cough.

'Ah,' he said, swallowing hard and looking from one to the other. 'Er—hallo, Blanche.'

'Oh, do you know each other?' said Amelia. 'I had no idea.'

'A little,' said Freddy carefully.

'Of course we know each other, darling,' said Blanche with a complacent smile. 'We're old friends, aren't we, Freddy? Why, I must have known you since you were—eighteen, was it?'

'Was it? I mean, was I? I don't remember, exactly,' said Freddy, darting a desperate glance at the door.

'You were already quite a man in many respects, and yet still such a child in others that I couldn't help but take you under my wing. How long ago it seems! And now look at you.'

'Er—' said Freddy. He was feeling uncomfortably hot, although it was a cold day, and was half-wondering how best to make his excuses and leave. Now that he thought back, he remembered Cynthia having said something about Mrs. Van Leeuwen being of the party that night, but he had been distracted by other things and the fact had not registered in his mind; nor had the idea that Amelia Drinkwater must be her daughter, although now that they were both standing before him, he could see the resemblance between them. This was all very awkward. With an enormous effort he managed to pull himself together and muster a semblance of good manners. 'You're looking very well too, Blanche,' he said. 'Not a day older than when I last saw you.'

'One does one's best,' said Blanche vaguely. She went to a little box that stood on a mirrored table and took out a cigarette. Freddy hastened forward to light it for her, and she directed a charming smile at him and threw herself onto a comfortable sofa, where she curled up like a cat and regarded them both with mild interest.

'So, then, am I to take it you wanted something?' she inquired.

'Yes,' said Amelia, who, fortunately, had not noticed a thing. 'Now, Mummy, Freddy's come to talk to you about last Thursday night, and it's terribly important that you answer his questions. His mother was there too, and we both quite agree that the murderer must be found before an innocent person is arrested.'

'Must we talk about it?' said Blanche, with a little *moue* of distaste. 'So unpleasant. I should far rather forget the whole thing. What does Cynthia say? No doubt she has strong opinions that she can't wait to bestow upon the public. Are we likely to read about it in that column of hers tomorrow?'

'I've no idea,' said Freddy, relieved to be brought to the matter at hand. 'I haven't seen much of her since last week. I expect she'll have the sense not to mention it, though. I don't suppose the police would be any too happy to read her thoughts—and anyway, the paper won't let her publish anything that might affect a trial.'

'Sensible of them,' said Blanche. 'Very well, what is it you want to know?'

'The police seem to think the poison was in the silver flask you all gave him for his birthday,' said Freddy.

'Oh, *that* again,' said Blanche. 'I told them I didn't see a thing. You know I never notice anything unless I'm particularly interested in it, darling.'

'But you did examine the flask,' said Freddy, ignoring the significant look she directed at him.

'Yes, and what an ugly object it was. I should never have bought anything so tasteless, myself.'

'Then it wasn't you who chose it?'

'Goodness, no! It was Nancy, I think. She agreed to see to it, and we all said we'd contribute. As a matter of fact, I was surprised when I saw it, because she'd mentioned something about getting him a pocket-watch. I should rather not have had anything to do with it, but one didn't feel as though one could refuse—especially since your mother was there, watching us all with those beady eyes of hers. I'm sorry, darling, I don't mean to offend, but you know she and I don't especially get along. At any rate, I only had the thing in my hand for about ten seconds, and then I passed it to Captain Atherton. Now *he* had a good look at it, I'm positive, because we'd both been expecting the pocket-watch, and he said he thought the flask was far more suitable for someone like Ticky, who *was* something of a drinker, it must be said.'

'I see,' said Freddy. 'Do you remember what Atherton did with it?'

'He passed it around the table. We all had a look at it.'

'And nobody drank out of it?'

'Certainly not,' said Blanche, with a disgusted look. 'What a dreadful idea! There's no saying where it might have been. I shouldn't have dreamt of putting it anywhere near my mouth.'

'Then any one of the party might have put poison in the flask,' said Freddy.

'That's what the police said,' agreed Blanche. 'And I dare say they're right.'

'It wasn't you, though?'

She threw back her head and let out a peal of laughter.

'Oh, darling, of course not! But how daring of you to ask me straight out. The police didn't, naturally, although I'm sure they were dying to.'

'Perhaps they didn't bother because they knew you wouldn't have admitted it even if you had done it,' said Freddy.

'That's true enough.'

'Who do you think killed him?'

'I've no idea,' said Blanche. 'And to be perfectly honest, I don't really care.'

'Mummy!' exclaimed Amelia.

'Oh, don't be so absurd, darling. You didn't like him either, and it's simply hypocritical to pretend you did.'

'I'm not pretending I liked him,' said Amelia, stung by the accusation. 'But murdering someone is a beastly thing to do, and you can't say it isn't. You're all under suspicion now, and while you might not care about your reputation, I do. I don't like to think of people talking about you behind their hands, and saying, "There goes Blanche Van Leeuwen—you know, the woman who's suspected of murdering Ticky Maltravers." It would be dreadful.'

'Oh, bother the man!' exclaimed Blanche suddenly. 'Why did he have to go and get himself murdered in the first place? Now the police are here, sneaking around, asking awkward questions of one, and there's no saying what they might discover. Ticky was a worm, right enough, but at least things were contained as long as he was alive.'

'What do you mean, contained?' said Amelia.

'Never mind,' said Blanche hurriedly. 'It's just my usual nonsense. Don't pay any attention. Listen, darling: the less said about this whole business, the better, and if you have any care for me at all you'll stay well out of it. The police don't need your help, anyway—quite the contrary, in fact. You'll just be in the way. Now,' she said, rising from her seat, 'the whole thing makes me sick, and I don't want to talk about it any more.' She refused to listen to her daughter's protests, but looked at Freddy as he stood up. 'I expect you understand,' she said.

'I think I do,' he replied.

She nodded, then paused at the door on the way out and threw him another look from under her eyelashes.

'Come to tea soon,' she said. 'It's been a long time. We can talk about the old days.'

'Er—' said Freddy uncomfortably. 'Well, perhaps—'

She smirked and left the room, and Freddy let out a silent sigh of relief.

'What did she mean?' said Amelia. 'What was contained? I don't understand what she was talking about.'

Freddy saw that he could not avoid the subject any longer.

'Perhaps I'd better explain,' he said.

CHAPTER TWELVE

ON FRIDAY AFTERNOON, Freddy found himself once more pacing up and down Caroline Terrace, wondering whether there were any way in which he could get hold of the evidence of Ticky's blackmail activities. Weaver had as good as admitted that the proof existed, but had said that it was not to be found in the house—and someone had already attempted to find it by burgling the place, so it was useless to try that again. For a few seconds, Freddy pondered the possibility of bribery—but no, that was no use either, for Weaver had an ample source of income that would last him many years if he chose, and what could Freddy offer him to match it? Very little, of course. And now there was not only Cynthia to think of (she was still lying low, and had not been found in any of her usual haunts that week, much to Freddy's exasperation), but also Blanche Van Leeuwen, the mother of Amelia Drinkwater. Amelia had been innocently unaware of Ticky's criminal enterprise until yesterday, and had been shocked to find out the truth, but she proclaimed stoutly that she was sure her mother had not been one of Ticky's victims—or, at least, had no secrets that could not be explained away by a misunderstanding. In view of his prior acquaintance with Mrs. Van Leeuwen, Freddy was careful to make no comment, and feared that Amelia was destined for disappointment at the very least; however, neither did he wish the blackmail to continue, and so he racked his brains, trying to find an answer to the problem. Of course, the surest way to find what he wanted was to watch Weaver day and night, for sooner or later surely the man would lead him to the hiding-place. However, Freddy had not the time to spare for that, since he had a job of work to do which required much of his attention. He had succeeded in arriving at his desk at half past eight every day that week, and had thus avoided the threatened carpeting from Mr. Bickerstaffe, but if he absented himself from the office too much, all his good work would be undone.

Occupied thus in reflection, Freddy almost missed the sight of Weaver himself coming out of number 24, Caroline Terrace, and walking off down the street. He was not looking about him, and Freddy immediately hastened after him, hoping to shadow him unobserved. Alas! It was not to be, for just then, a young woman coming the other way addressed Weaver with some slight salutation, and when he looked up to reply he glanced around and saw Freddy. He smirked, shook his head, and hurried off. Freddy saw that his attempt would be useless, and grimaced to himself. He was frowning at the young woman and administering epithets to her in his mind when he suddenly realized he knew her from somewhere. After a moment's thought, he remembered: it was the girl he had caught rifling through a cupboard at Marjorie Belcher's charity reception.

'Hallo, hallo,' he said, as she drew near him. 'If it isn't the teetotal revolutionary. How are the war preparations going?'

She looked up, recognized him and stopped.

'Oh, it's you,' she said. 'What do you want?'

She spoke without rancour, and Freddy examined her with interest, for she looked completely different from when he had last seen her. On that day she had been dressed in a drab, dowdy frock and scuffed shoes, her hair flattened against her head and her skin bare of ornament, as befitted the rôle she had been called upon to play that afternoon at the grand reception. Now before him stood a smart young woman of seemingly quite a different class, for her attire was new and fashionable— not to say bohemian—while her hair curled and shone, her lips were coloured the deepest red, and her expression was all knowingness. Even her accent, which had been pure East End the last time he had spoken to her, seemed to have slid up a class or two. Had it not been for her dark, heavy eyebrows, in fact, he might not have recognized her at all.

'Do you know that man?' asked Freddy.

Her mouth curled.

'I've met him before,' she said. 'Friend of yours, is he?'

'Certainly not,' said Freddy. 'But I'm interested in knowing more about him.'

'Oh? What do you want to know?'

'Where did you meet him?'

'Sir Aldridge Featherstone's. A girl I know is in service there, and I go in to help sometimes, when there's a big dinner or evening-party. He was there once, and my friend pointed him out to me. Very free with his hands, she said.'

'And was he?' said Freddy.

'I don't know,' said the girl. 'I didn't let him get close enough to find out. But we exchanged polite remarks once or twice, which is why I said hallo to him in the street just now. Why? What have you got on him?'

'Why should you think I have anything on him?' said Freddy, intrigued by her choice of phrase.

'Because I know a bad 'un when I see one. Go on, then, what's he done?'

'He's a blackmailer,' said Freddy.

She showed no surprise.

'Yes, that makes sense,' she said. 'He looks the sneaky sort. Listens at doors and reads other people's letters, does he?'

'Almost certainly.'

'It's a nasty thing to do. Someone ought to thump him one. I can arrange it for you if you don't want to do it yourself. How much has he got out of you? I can get that back too, if you like.'

'Oh, it's not me,' said Freddy hurriedly, taken aback at the matter-of-fact way in which she had offered to solve his problem.

'Who, then?'

'Some friends of mine. It's not quite as simple as that, though. I don't suppose you've been following the Maltravers case in the papers?'

'Chap who was poisoned at dinner?' she said after a moment's thought.

'The very same,' said Freddy. 'Maltravers was the real blackmailer. Weaver was his man, and merely inherited the business from him.'

She stared, then laughed.

'So this Maltravers was bumped off by one of his friends, I take it?' she said. 'And now his servant's willing to take the risk that they'll come after him now? Rather him than me, I say.'

'Quite,' said Freddy. 'Still, that doesn't alter the fact that at present he has a large number of people in his power.'

'And you want to stop him? How are you going to do that?'

'I'm not sure,' said Freddy. 'But it seems to me the first step is to find whatever dirt he has on his victims and get it off him.'

She immediately turned and looked up appraisingly at the windows of number 24, Caroline Terrace, then glanced around at the street itself.

'Can't get in in broad daylight,' she said. 'It's too exposed. What's round the back?'

'Someone's already tried,' said Freddy. 'The place was burgled on Monday. Whoever it was didn't find what he was looking for—I can tell you that for certain, because Weaver told me so. He as good as said that he keeps the evidence somewhere else. I was about to follow him just now when he spotted me.'

'Was that my fault? Sorry,' she said. 'I didn't mean to spoil everything.'

'You weren't to know,' said Freddy.

'What'll you do now?' she said. 'You won't find out where it is without spying on him, will you? And you can't do that without standing in the street all day, but he'll see you if you do that.'

'I don't have time to do it anyway,' said Freddy. 'I'm wanted at work at least some of the time.'

'I could do it if you like,' she said. She pointed at a house diagonally across the way from number 24. 'That's my berth at the moment. I reckon I'll be there for another couple of weeks, at least.'

'In service?' said Freddy.

'Not I,' she replied with a snort. 'I do it when it suits me once in a while, but never for long. No,' she went on, 'I'm by way of being an artists' model—for now, at any rate. The two young chaps who live in the house have more money than they know what to do with, and they like to dabble, but to describe them as artists is a bit much, if you ask me. Still, the work's easy. I can lie there and stare out of the window for hours on end and get paid for it.'

'Ah, I understand,' said Freddy. 'You'll be able to see when Weaver comes out of the house.'

'That's right,' she said.

'But pardon me, it's not as though you can run out and chase him down the street if you see him, is it? I mean to say, what will your painter chappies think? And I presume you work in a state of—er—undress. Society tends to look askance upon that sort of thing in public, don't you know?'

'My painters won't mind,' she said. 'We have an understanding. And I can get dressed in eighteen seconds flat, down to coat and hat. I've timed it.'

Freddy forbore to ask the nature of the circumstances which had obliged her to acquire this ability, but instead regarded her thoughtfully. He had been half-thinking of employing some boy or other to watch the house, but now here was this young woman, offering to do it for him, and he was not the sort to turn down an opportunity if it presented itself. She was a strange girl, and he could not make her out, but he decided to risk it.

'Do you think you could find out where he keeps the information?' he said at last.

She shrugged.

'I can try. I can't promise anything, but I'll do what I can.'

'All right then,' said Freddy. 'You're on.' He tore a sheet from his notebook and scribbled something on it. 'Here's where you can find me. If I'm not there, try me at the offices of the *Clarion*. That's where I work.'

She glanced at the paper.

'Right you are, *Mister* Pilkington-Soames,' she said. 'Let's see what I can do. I like an adventure, and this looks as if it might be a good one.'

'I could do without that sort of adventure myself,' he said. 'You haven't told me your name, by the way.'

'It's Valentina Sangiacomo.'

'Ah, I thought there was something foreign about you, despite the accent,' said Freddy. 'Italian, is it?'

'That and a few other countries,' she said, but did not enlarge further.

'Well, Miss Sangiacomo, I suppose I'd better give you something on account.'

'Yes, I suppose you had,' she said, and to his astonishment held up something he recognized immediately as his own pocket-book. She opened it, selected a note, and handed it back to him. 'This'll do to start with. You can pay me more later.'

'What the devil—' he said, patting his pocket and finding it empty. 'Why, you little—'

'Take it as a free lesson,' she said with perfect unconcern. 'You ought to look after your things more carefully. Anyone else wouldn't have given it back. Count it if you like. I only took the ten.'

He did so, and found she was telling the truth.

'How do I know you won't keep the information if you find it?' he said.

'You don't, but I won't. Blackmail's a sneak's trade, and I'm not a sneak. And neither are you, which is why I offered to help you. What time is it?' she said suddenly, and craned her head to look at his watch. He put his hand on it instinctively, for it was rather a valuable one. 'I'd better go. You'll hear from me soon. Goodbye—and watch your pockets!'

And with that she tucked his ten shillings into the front of her dress, flashed him her radiant smile and walked off.

CHAPTER THIRTEEN

I F FREDDY HAD had any thoughts as to how best to recover the information Ticky Maltravers had held about his victims, they certainly had not entailed employing a young woman of questionable character to spy on Ticky's manservant, Weaver. But now that the agreement had been made, he was not at all sure whether he had done the right thing, for this Valentina Sangiacomo seemed to be something of a law unto herself, and despite her professed dislike of blackmail, there was no saying whether she might not decide to keep the information if she found it—always supposing she did what she had been engaged to do at all, in fact. Still, the deed was done now, and all he could do was wait to hear from her. In the meantime, he had yet to speak to his mother about the missing silver flask. Since her house was just around the corner, he went and knocked at the door, although without much hope of finding her there. Mrs. Hanbury answered.

'Hallo, Mrs. H,' he said. 'Is my mother at home?'

She did not have time to reply before Cynthia herself came out into the entrance-hall, saw him and gave a little squeak of fear. She covered it up immediately and smiled briskly.

'Hallo, darling,' she said. 'Where on earth have you been? I've been wanting to talk to you for days about the dinner-party next week. Now, you will come, won't you? I've already spoken for you, so you'd better not forget to turn up, as you did last time. It was very embarrassing, especially since I'd been boasting to Dinah Hepworth about what a devoted and well-behaved son you are. You know all that trouble they had with their Edward—heaven knows how much they had to pay to get the girl to keep quiet, but I said at the time he wasn't the sort to make a success of being a vicar, and I was right, wasn't I? I told Dinah how lucky I was that you're not generally the type to get into a scrape, but then I had to think of all sorts of excuses as to why you hadn't turned up. Anyway, she's coming again this time, so it's probably best you keep to general subjects—no politics, or anything like that. And *don't* mention the incident with the suit of armour at Great-Uncle Algy's funeral. I know it was all a misunderstanding, but Aunt Ernestine was rather cross, because she'd picked a tremendously inspiring text for the reading, and the noise drowned it out completely. Anyway, I must dash. You won't make a mess, will you?'

'Oh, no you don't,' said Freddy, as she attempted to sidle past him and out into the street. 'Don't think you can get away that easily. I want a word with you.'

'Why, darling, whatever's the matter?' she said, opening her eyes wide.

'You know perfectly well what's the matter,' said Freddy. He lowered his voice and glanced around, to make sure Mrs. Hanbury was not within earshot. 'What have you done with the flask?'

'Which flask?'

'Ticky's flask, of course. I know you took it. What did you do with it?'

'Why, I—er—' she said nervously. 'Look, I don't have time for this at the moment. Do you mind awfully if we talk about it later? I was supposed to be in Bond Street half an hour ago, and it's almost impossible to find a taxi at this time of day.'

'Yes, I do mind,' said Freddy. 'You silly woman, can't you see that if the police suspect for a second you took it, then you'll be arrested for murder?'

'Nonsense,' said Cynthia. 'The police know perfectly well that I had nothing to do with the murder. We had a pleasant little chat earlier in the week, and I told them Ticky was perfectly all right when I left him, and they didn't give the slightest sign that they'd guessed what really happened.'

'But they're looking for the flask,' said Freddy. 'There's no other way Ticky could have been killed. The poison was in the flask, and they know he had it when he was in the taxi. Quite frankly, I'm surprised they haven't been here to search the house yet. Now, confess it: you took it from his pocket, didn't you?'

She lowered her eyes.

'Oh, very well,' she admitted at last. 'Yes, I took it. But you must understand, darling, that I was in a dreadful fright, and I didn't know what to do. I mean, what was I to think when he drank from the flask, shouted "Poison!" and then died? First I was terrified they'd arrest me, and after that I started to think that even if they didn't—even if I managed to convince them that it was nothing to do with me—they'd start snooping about, and find out about the blackmail, and then where would I be? So in the end I decided it was safest to pretend there was no flask at all, and hope they wouldn't realize it was murder.'

'But they were bound to realize it once we moved the body,' said Freddy. 'I only wish you'd called the police to start with, instead of dragging him all over the place and rifling through his pockets.'

'*I* didn't drag him all over the place,' said Cynthia. 'I believe that was you.'

'Only because you took advantage of me,' said Freddy indignantly. 'I'd never have dreamed of doing it if I'd been in my right mind. I hope I'd have had the sense to leave him where he was and call for help without touching anything. Listen: if it weren't for the fact that I might be arrested as an accessory at any moment, I'd leave you to stew, so you ought to think yourself lucky that one of us, at least, understands what a sticky position you're in. As long as you have that flask you're in terrible danger, and you were an idiot to steal it in the first place.'

'All right, perhaps I was,' she said crossly. 'But there's no need to be so superior. When was the last time someone dropped dead unexpectedly in front of *you*? I can't help it if I'm not very good at keeping my head in an emergency, and I can see now it was probably a mistake, but I only did what I thought was best at the time.'

'Where is it now?'

'I put it behind the wardrobe,' she said reluctantly.

'Behind the wardrobe? That's the first place they'll look. You'd better give it to me.'

'Yes, yes,' she said eagerly. 'And you'll throw it in the river for me, won't you darling?'

'I might if the police didn't already know about it,' said Freddy. 'But it's too late for that, I'm afraid. They do know about it, and if they never find it then you'll all be under suspicion forever. It's probably still got poison in it, and they'll need it for evidence.'

'Evidence of what?' said Cynthia. 'They still won't know who put the poison in there. But if we get rid of it we can pretend the whole thing never happened. The police will never know, and we can all go on as we were before.'

'Don't be silly,' said Freddy. 'A man is dead. I know he was ghastly, but the police don't care about that. They're not just going to go away. They'll keep on asking awkward questions until they find out who killed him, and at the moment I'm pretty certain they think it was you.'

'But it wasn't!' exclaimed Cynthia, wide-eyed. 'I promise you it wasn't.'

Freddy regarded his mother. In spite of his own misgivings and her idiotic behaviour, he found he believed her.

'Then we need to let the police find out who really did do it,' he said. 'And they can't do that without all the evidence.'

'Oh, very well then,' she said at last. 'I suppose I'd better go and get it.'

She turned and went upstairs, and returned a minute or two later with the article in question wrapped in a handkerchief.

'I didn't touch it,' she said. 'Finger-prints, you see.'

'Then you showed *some* sense, at least,' said Freddy. He held it in the handkerchief, being careful not to touch it himself, and examined it with interest. There was not much to see; it was a flask like any other, although clearly rather expensive.

'Real silver,' he said, observing the hall-mark.

'Five pounds eighteen and six, it cost,' said Cynthia in disgust. 'Nancy sent Ann to Harrods for it. I don't know what possessed her to spend so much. And she had his initials put on it, too.'

'So I see,' said Freddy, looking at the large N and M engraved with a flourish on the convex side of the flask. He gave it a little shake.

'About a quarter full, I should say,' he said. 'How much brandy was in there to start with?'

'I've no idea,' said Cynthia. 'Not terribly much, I imagine. The bottle was still nearly full after they'd finished decanting it. I don't think Denis or Captain Atherton were particularly happy. I heard them muttering something together about its being a waste of good Cognac.'

Freddy unscrewed the stopper, then approached his nose to the neck and sniffed gingerly.

'Do be careful, darling,' said Cynthia. 'We don't want you to drop dead too.'

'I don't think it's possible to die from inhaling nicotine,' said Freddy. 'At least, I hope not.'

'Can you smell anything?' said Cynthia.

'Only brandy. I won't take a sip, though.' He replaced the stopper and put the flask in his pocket, still wrapped in the handkerchief. 'Now, all we have to do is think of a way to get it to the police.'

'But how? We can't simply hand it to them.'

'No, the fact that you took it will look extremely suspicious. I'm certain they're already looking for an excuse to arrest you. I shall have to think of something. Perhaps we can say he left it in the taxi.'

'That's no good,' said Cynthia. 'The police have already found it and searched it.'

'Perhaps they didn't search hard enough,' said Freddy. 'Now, listen. Is there anything you haven't told me? I mean to say, you didn't steal anything else, did you? I should hate to get you out of this fix, only for you to be arrested when they find out you took his cigarette-case and his watch, too.'

'You talk as though I had a habit of scavenging from dead bodies,' said Cynthia. 'What on earth would I want with his cigarette-case? I have one of my own.'

'And you're quite sure there's nothing else you haven't mentioned?'

'Quite sure,' said Cynthia firmly.

'Well, there'd better not be,' said Freddy. 'Because if I find out you're hiding anything, I shall have no choice but to tell Father about what's been going on.'

'You're an undutiful son,' said Cynthia petulantly.

'No, but look here—can't you tell him yourself? I mean to say, he's going to get an awful shock if the police do arrest you. Wouldn't it be better to prepare him a little, perhaps?'

'No!' said Cynthia. 'He wouldn't be at all pleased. There's no reason he should find out about any of this as long as we're careful. He's been nervous about all that sort of thing ever since the Gipsy's Mile business, and he wasn't any too happy when the police turned up the other day.'

'I take it you haven't told him about the blackmail, then?'

'Goodness, no! He'd be terribly cross.'

'You ought to, you know. If you don't, you're going to find yourself paying out even more money,' said Freddy. 'By the way—that's another thing I wanted to speak to you about. I saw Weaver on Monday. Have you heard from him?'

'Oh, Weaver!' she said. 'I'd completely forgotten about him. That beastly little man. I had a telephone-call from him the other day, to say that he wanted to speak to me about continuing the payments. He even had the cheek to demand I spread the word for him, and that I go to Caroline Terrace to pay him, to save him the trouble of coming to collect. Imagine that! *He* summoned *me*! It's all most vexing—especially since I thought you were going to fix all that for me.'

Freddy grimaced.

'I did my best, but the evidence isn't in the house,' he said. 'Weaver told me so.'

'Bother,' said Cynthia. 'Can you find it?'

'I'm doing what I can, but in the meantime I really think you ought to tell Father.'

'Certainly not,' she said stubbornly. 'I've kept it secret all this time. Think of what a waste of money it would be if I told him now.'

Freddy had no reply to such an obstinate refusal to look at the facts logically.

'Besides,' she went on, 'I've talked to Nancy, and she agrees it's best not to say anything.'

'Oh, you've talked to Nancy, have you?' said Freddy. 'What is it, a sort of blackmail victims' trade union?'

'Don't be silly, darling,' she said. 'We're friends, that's all. Friends talk to one another.'

'What does she have to hide?' said Freddy curiously. 'I suppose you can't tell me.'

'Oh, nothing much,' said Cynthia. 'Just a little matter of excessive high spirits. But she doesn't want Mrs. Belcher to find out about it. Or Denis, for that matter.'

'I believe you're rather enjoying all this,' said Freddy suddenly.

'Of course I'm not enjoying it,' said Cynthia. 'But I refuse to take it too seriously, either. After all, nobody is really going to arrest any of us, are they? Our sort don't get arrested. Why, we're in the papers all the time. People want to know about our clothes, and our hair, and which parties we've been to, and which people we've spoken to. Nobody could possibly believe that any of us would murder someone. That's not the sort of thing we do. It's only common people who get arrested—you know, the sort who hit other people over the head and steal their money. We're nothing like that, are we?'

'I should agree with you if it weren't for the fact that we both know at least two people who have been arrested for murder in the past,' said Freddy. 'If you're relying on your family name and your reputation at the *Clarion* to save you, then you needn't bother. The police are just as likely to suspect you as they are anyone else, and your important connections won't help you one bit if they decide you did it. They'll hang you just as happily as they would the chap who hit the other chap over the head.'

'I do wish you wouldn't say things like that,' said Cynthia, wincing. 'It all sounds terribly unpleasant.'

'But it's true, and the sooner you realize it the better. Now, listen: I shall do what I can to make sure the police never find out you took the flask, but you mustn't say a word about it, or it'll all have been for nothing.'

'I shall be as silent as the grave,' she promised.

'Good. Now you have nothing to fear when they turn up here with a search warrant.'

'They won't do that, will they?' she said in surprise.

Freddy was about to reply when there was a knock at the door.

'Good afternoon, Mrs. Pilkington-Soames,' said Inspector Entwistle, when Cynthia answered. 'I'm sorry to bother you, but I'm afraid we're going to have to search your house. I have here a warrant.'

He stepped into the entrance-hall in the manner of one who was not about to be put off. Sergeant Bird and two other men followed, slightly more apologetically.

'Goodness me!' said Cynthia, taken aback. 'Well, I'm sure you're very welcome to look around, although I can't think what you might be looking for.'

'It's the silver flask, isn't it?' said Freddy. 'I told you they'd come and look for it. I only hope you haven't shoved it behind the wardrobe, or something.'

'Freddy!' snapped Cynthia. 'I don't know where he gets his sense of humour from,' she said, turning to the inspector. 'It's certainly not from me.'

Entwistle smiled briefly, and started giving orders to the men. Freddy turned to Sergeant Bird.

'Look here, sergeant,' he said. 'Are you quite sure the flask wasn't in Ticky's possession? What about the taxi?'

'We searched the cab and it wasn't there,' said Bird.

'It was a valuable thing, wasn't it?' said Freddy. 'Silver. Something of a temptation to a taxi-driver, don't you think?'

'Are you suggesting he found it and kept it?'

'Well, far be it from me to cast aspersions on the man's character without any foundation for it, but it's possible,' said Freddy. He pretended to think. 'I wonder, might I speak to him? I might be able to persuade him to confide in me, since I'm not a policeman.'

'I don't see why not,' said Bird, after a moment's reflection. 'I reckon you'll be wasting your time, though.' He consulted his notebook. 'This is the chap,' he said. 'He works around Holborn.'

Freddy made a note.

'Thanks,' he said. 'I'll see what I can do.'

'You'd be better off getting back to your own work,' said Bird.

'Oh, but this is much more interesting. And if something comes of it I shall have a scoop, and Mr. Bickerstaffe will shower me with praise and hold a dinner in my honour.'

'Funny thing, this reporting business,' said Bird.

'Oh, it is,' Freddy assured him. 'You'll be all right, won't you?' he said to Cynthia, who was starting to fidget.

'I think so, darling,' she said. 'You'd better go. I'll speak to you later.'

She opened the front door and ushered him out hurriedly, and he made his escape with the flask in his pocket.

Chapter Fourteen

THE TAXI-DRIVER, a morose and taciturn man of fifty, was having a bite to eat at a slightly grubby establishment near Kingsway in between shifts, and glanced up without curiosity when a young man strolled in who appeared altogether too well looked-after to be frequenting that sort of place.

'I'm looking for a Bert Evans,' announced Freddy to the place at large.

One or two voices directed him to the table in the corner, and he headed in the direction indicated.

'Awfully sorry to bother you while you're eating,' he said, 'but I'd like a word with you. You don't mind if I sit?' He did so without waiting for a reply, turned his head to right and left as though to be sure they could not be overheard, then leaned forward and said in a low voice, 'I've come to warn you that you may be in a spot of trouble.'

'Trouble? What kind of trouble?' said Bert, surprised.

'I gather you had a visit from the police the other day,' said Freddy.

'What of it?' said Bert.

'I understand they were looking for something in particular. A silver flask.'

'That's what they said, and they looked and didn't find it,' said Bert. 'I told them they wouldn't.'

'Did you? How did you know?'

''Cause the chap had it in 'is hand when he got out, didn't he?'

'Are you sure of that?'

'Sure as I can be,' said Bert.

Freddy coughed delicately.

'The thing is, I'm not sure the police believe you.'

Bert squinted at him suspiciously.

'What do you mean? And who are you to be telling me this?'

Freddy produced his press card.

'Pilkington-Soames of the *Clarion*,' he said.

'Oh, one of these reporter fellers, are you?' said Bert, unimpressed.

'Yes. I'm following the Maltravers case—the man who died, you know—and I'm afraid the police may be making rather a clumsy fist of it. I'm good pals with the sergeant who's been assigned to the case—not a bad fellow, all told, but somewhat held back by his inspector, who's a narrow-minded sort, and inclined to jump to conclusions. Now, I was speaking to the sergeant this morning, and he said it's of vital importance that they find this flask, as they're certain it contained the poison, but they've looked everywhere and haven't found a trace of it. That's when he mentioned you.'

'Me?'

'Yes. One doesn't like to ruin a man's dinner, but I think I ought to warn you that they suspect you of having filched the thing yourself.'

'What?' said Bert in alarm. 'But I never. I'm an honest man, I am.'

Freddy gave him a conspiratorial look.

'Oh, we're all honest up to a point,' he said. 'I mean to say, I'd never dream of breaking into someone's house and stealing the Spode, but I shouldn't like anyone to look too closely at my expense-account. And if I happened to find a ten shilling note lying on the ground, I can't absolutely promise that I'd look for its owner. I expect you understand what I mean. Don't people leave things lying around in your cab once in a while?'

'Sometimes,' said Bert. 'But I always hand 'em in.'

'What? Always?' said Freddy. 'Do you mean to say you've never kept the odd umbrella?'

'Well—' said Bert uncomfortably.

'You see? And yet I'm quite sure you don't consider yourself a thief.'

'That's 'cause I ain't,' said Bert, outraged. 'I never took the flask.'

'A pretty silver affair, it was,' said Freddy, unperturbed. 'It cost at least five pounds new, I understand. I don't know how long they give you for that sort of thing these days. Six months, perhaps? I suppose you might get a sympathetic judge, but I shouldn't like to rely on it.'

'Here, now,' said Bert, increasingly dismayed. 'They can't arrest me. They've no proof of anything.'

'No, but they can make your life fairly difficult. I don't suppose you relish the thought of the police hanging around the Public Carriage Office, asking awkward questions about your good character or otherwise.'

'I've never had any trouble with the Office,' said Bert. 'And I don't want any, either.'

'Then perhaps you ought to make a clean breast of it,' said Freddy. 'Come, now, what did you do with it?'

'Nothing, I tell you!' exclaimed Bert. 'The chap had it when he got into my cab, and he still had it when he got out as far as I know.'

'As far as you know? Then you didn't see him holding it when he got out, as you said?'

'I thought I did,' said Bert. 'But you've got me that muddled I don't know what I saw now. All I know is that I didn't take it.'

'All right, then, if you didn't take it, might he have left it in the taxi?'

'But the police looked for it.'

'There's always the chance they missed it. They work in such a hurry that they can be a bit careless, you see. What if it's still there?'

'D'you think so?' said Bert, with dawning hope.

'Why don't we go and have a look?' said Freddy. 'Let's go now. They might turn up at any moment, and if they're bent on arresting you then they won't be interested in listening to you until you get to court, and you don't want that.'

Bert shoved a last forkful of food into his mouth and stood up.

'We better had, then,' he said. 'Cab's round the corner.'

At the rank on Kingsway, a little cluster of boys gathered to watch the scene, and amused themselves with a series of impertinent comments at the sight of Bert, whose hind-quarters were the only thing visible, for his front half was inside the cab, rummaging about. At intervals, grimy old cushions and a variety of personal belongings were tossed out onto the pavement, eliciting many giggles and rude remarks. At last, Bert emerged and scratched his head.

'Nothing,' he said.

'Have you looked everywhere?' said Freddy.

'Short of taking the thing apart, yes, I have,' said Bert.

'I don't suppose it got wedged on the running-board under the door,' suggested Freddy.

Bert shook his head.

'No,' continued Freddy, examining his hands. 'It would be too ridiculous for it to be anywhere on the outside of the car. Although I have heard of things getting themselves trapped behind the spare wheel. It's hardly worth looking, though. It certainly won't be there.'

Bert came around to the back of the car and peered down behind the spare wheel.

'Oh!' he said in surprise. 'It's here! I told you I didn't take it.'

'By Jove, are you sure?' exclaimed Freddy, who had planted the flask there himself not twenty minutes ago. He leapt up, and was just in time to prevent Bert from reaching into the narrow space and pulling it out. 'Better not,' he said. 'Finger-prints.'

'What?' said Bert.

'If you touch it, you'll put finger-prints on it, and the police will think you took it but had a change of heart at the last minute. Use a handkerchief.'

The flask was removed carefully from its hiding-place.

'Now, how on earth did it get there?' said Bert.

'Most odd,' said Freddy, then paused as though struck by a sudden thought. 'Wasn't Maltravers a little the worse for wear when he got out of the car? I expect he staggered against it and dropped the flask down there as he passed.'

'Well I never,' said Bert.

'You'd better take it to Scotland Yard as soon as you can,' said Freddy.

'Can't you do it?'

'Oh, no,' said Freddy. 'We'll both get into trouble if they find out I warned you. Either they'll think you really did steal it, then persuaded me to hand it in with some sob-story or other, or they'll think we cooked the whole thing up together for the purposes of news. Inspector Entwistle doesn't think much of the press, you see. He seems to have the strangest idea that I make up my stories. No; much better not to bring me into it at all, then you can take the credit for having found it for them.'

'All right, then,' said Bert. 'Does that mean you're not going to put it in the paper?'

He seemed a little disappointed.

'Oh, I'll put it in the paper, all right, but not until the police say so. Don't worry, I'll be sure to name you as the man who found the missing murder weapon.'

'I'd like that,' said Bert. 'I've never seen my name in print before.'

'Well, keep a look-out in the *Clarion*, and I'm certain you'll see it before long,' said Freddy. 'Now, don't forget—take it to Scotland Yard straightaway.'

He bade the taxi-driver a cheery goodbye and headed off down Kingsway. As soon as he was out of sight he let out a great sigh of relief and half a whistle.

'Let's hope that's the end of *that*,' he said to himself. 'Mother ought to be in the clear now—at least as far as all this business of tampering with the body is concerned. With any luck the police will forget all that and concern themselves with finding out who killed Ticky.' He frowned. 'I wonder who *did* do it, though?' he went on. 'I suppose it must have been one of them, but whoever it was did a good job of getting the poison in there discreetly. They must all have been pretty drunk not to have noticed it. Still, one would have thought the waiters at least might have seen something. I wonder—'

Here he paused, as a thought passed fleetingly through his mind. What was it, now? Something to do with the flask. Was it something his mother had said? He could not remember, but he was sure an idea had come to him just then. They had originally intended to buy Ticky a pocket-watch. Now, why was that significant? For it *was* significant, he was sure. But why? The thought seemed determined to elude him for the present. Perhaps it would come back to him later. In the meantime, he turned his mind back to the situation at hand. It looked as though whoever had committed the murder had done so for nothing, now that Weaver had taken over the concern. Freddy did not envy Ticky's manservant one bit.

'He's a brave one, after what happened to his master,' he said to himself. 'Or foolhardy, I should say. I shouldn't like to be in his shoes if someone really is going around murdering black-mailers. He'd better watch his step or he's likely to be next.'

And so saying, he returned to the *Clarion*'s offices, where he was late with a moralizing piece on the advisability of honesty and plain dealing as the foundations for a happy life.

CHAPTER FIFTEEN

INSPECTOR ENTWISTLE PICKED his way gingerly among the mess in the sitting-room of number 24, Caroline Terrace, and peered out of the window. It was Sunday morning, and the street was quiet. He turned back and looked at Dr. Ingleby as he crouched over the prostrate figure of Weaver, who was lying face-down, the handle of a large knife protruding from his back.

'Straight to the heart, I'd say,' said Ingleby. 'He probably didn't feel a thing.'

'Not much blood,' said Sergeant Bird, who had been watching the doctor dispassionately.

'No,' said Ingleby. 'It obviously didn't hit any major blood vessels. Just a fraction of an inch to the right or left, however, and it would be a different story.'

'When did it happen?' said Entwistle.

'Some time last night, at a guess. All the signs are that he's been dead a good twelve hours or so.'

'Do you think it's the same person who broke in before, sir?' said Bird, addressing the inspector.

'Could be,' said Entwistle. 'Weaver said they didn't take anything the first time, so perhaps they came back for another try, and he happened to be in the way.' He frowned, and regarded the rug, which had been turned back. 'Here's something queer, though,' he said. 'They looked under here last time. And in that chest over there. Do you remember, Bird? Weaver complained that they'd scratched one of the drawers.'

'Oh, yes,' said Bird. 'That's true. I see what you mean. Why would they look in the same place twice, if they didn't find whatever they were looking for the first time?'

'Rather a waste of effort,' said Entwistle. 'Unless, of course, this is someone quite different.'

'Seems a bit too much of a coincidence, don't you think, sir? I mean to say, is it likely that two different people would break into the house within a week?'

'Not in the normal way of things, but it's pretty clear this wasn't a normal burglary.'

'Then you don't think Weaver was killed when he interrupted the thief?'

Entwistle shook his head.

'Any indications of a struggle?' he said to Ingleby.

'Not that I can see,' said the doctor. 'It's a clean blow, and you can see he wasn't running away by the direction he's facing. Naturally, I can't comment until I've done a proper examination of the body, but if you want my immediate opinion, I should say this was a quite deliberate killing. I think he turned his back for a second and paid the price for it.'

Just then, P. C. Johnson entered the room.

'We can't find any signs of a break-in, sir,' he said.

'Are you sure you've looked properly?' said Bird. 'After all, you missed the flask.'

'I looked everywhere in that taxi,' said Johnson with some heat, for he had been defending himself against this charge since Friday. 'I know I looked down behind the spare wheel. I reckon the taxi-driver had it all along.'

'Well, if he did, he had the sense not to put his finger-prints all over it,' said Bird. He had his own suspicions as to what had really happened to the flask, but since Bert Evans was sticking firmly to his story, and had denied having been influenced by anybody, there was little to be done about it at present. 'At least that's something. And lucky for him he didn't take it into his head to drink from it, or we'd have three murders to think about, not two.'

'Is it certain that's where the poison was, then, sir?' said Johnson.

'I'll say,' said Bird. 'There was enough nicotine in it to kill a man three times over. Now, are you sure nobody's broken in?'

'Yes, sir. All the windows are shut, and there's no indication that any of them have been forced.'

Entwistle and Bird looked at each other.

'Then it must have been someone he knew,' said Entwistle. 'He must have let them in through the front door.'

'One of the crowd from Babcock's, do you suppose?' said Bird.

'It must be,' said Entwistle. 'Although I'm damned if I can see why. Still, there must be some connection between the two murders. It can't possibly be a coincidence.'

'Are we to assume that the person who killed Weaver is the same as the person who killed Maltravers?' said Bird.

'Oh, yes, I think we must—at least until we get evidence to the contrary. But what was the motive?'

'Money's a popular one,' suggested Bird.

'Ah, yes,' said Entwistle. 'The bank book. Maltravers was depositing regular sums of three or four hundred pounds a month into his bank account. All in cash. Where did it come from? He didn't have a job that we know of, or a private income, although he was investing some of the money rather tidily in funds.'

'Drugs?' said Bird. 'It's quite a disease of the upper classes, I understand. Someone has to supply the stuff.'

'Perhaps. Although we didn't find any evidence of it when we searched the house the other day. What else?'

'Blackmail?' said Bird.

'That seems more likely to me,' said the inspector. 'It seems to fit with the deposits to his account. He'd collect the payments in cash, then take them to the bank once he'd amassed a certain sum. That way nobody could say where the money had come from.'

'But if he knew things to people's disadvantage, and was demanding money off them in return for his silence, wouldn't he have kept evidence?' said Bird. 'I mean to say, it's easier to blackmail someone if you have proof of what they've been up to. But we didn't find anything like that the other day.'

'True,' said Entwistle. 'Still, it would explain the burglaries, since once Maltravers was dead his victims were bound to come looking for whatever he had on them. I wonder if it really is here in the house. Weaver said nothing had been taken after the burglary on Monday, but perhaps whoever broke in didn't search hard enough. Let's have another look. You go through those drawers, and I'll search his writing-desk. They've finished taking photographs and dusting for finger-prints, haven't they? Are you done, Ingleby?'

'Yes, I think so,' said the doctor. 'I'll take him out of your way now and let you get on. Johnson, go and fetch Lamb, and bring the stretcher.'

There was some little ado as the mortal remains of Weaver were carried carefully from the house and taken away, then Entwistle and Bird settled down to search through Ticky Maltravers' personal effects, in an attempt to find out exactly what had prompted someone to murder both him and his manservant within the space of ten days. For a while there was no sound but the opening and closing of drawers and the rustle of papers, then at last Inspector Entwistle gave a great sigh and slammed shut the desk.

'Nothing,' he said. 'What about you?'

'Nothing much,' said Bird. 'Only this. What do you think it is?'

He handed his superior a letter. Entwistle glanced at it, then read it more closely.

'It's a statement of account from a clippings bureau,' he said. 'Interesting.'

'A clippings bureau? Isn't that one of those places that cuts out stories from the paper and sends them to you?'

'That's right,' said Entwistle.

'Do you think he was collecting dirt on his friends?' said Bird.

'It looks rather like it,' said the inspector. He looked back at the letter. 'We'd better speak to these people and find out what they sent him.'

'It's an ugly job,' remarked Bird. 'Prying into people's secrets, I mean.'

'It can't be helped,' said Entwistle. 'We don't have much in the way of evidence—only a silver flask with brandy and nicotine in it, and no way of knowing how the nicotine got in there—so the next step is to find out who had a motive.'

'It's just a pity they passed the flask around the table,' said Bird. 'They couldn't have confused things more if they'd tried. Why, the thing's covered in finger-prints. Any of them might have done it.'

'Presumably only one of them did, though.'

'And we still don't know who moved the body, or why, or where from,' went on Bird. 'It's a puzzle, all right.'

'Well, we won't solve it by sitting here,' said Entwistle. 'Let's search the house again. And this time, look for loose floor-boards. If Maltravers was a blackmailer then there must be something in writing.'

———————

AMELIA DRINKWATER AND her mother had just returned from their Sunday walk in the Park, when the telephone rang. Blanche had taken her customary position before the looking-glass, and was busy adjusting her hair after removing her hat, so Amelia went to answer it. Blanche listened with half an ear, then stopped what she was doing and turned her head slightly at the sound of her daughter's voice, which was raised in astonishment. Two minutes later Amelia came in.

'That was Larry,' she said. 'Weaver's been found murdered!'

'Who?' said Blanche.

'Weaver. Ticky's man.'

Blanche stared at her daughter for a moment, then turned back to the glass and went on with what she had been doing.

'Was that his name?' she said carelessly. 'Well, I can't say I'm surprised. What was it this time? A knock on the head? A bullet to the brain?'

'He was stabbed,' said Amelia.

'At home?'

'Yes. The police think he may have disturbed a burglar, because the place was in a mess.'

'Nonsense,' said Blanche. 'A burglar, indeed! If the police think that then they're more stupid than I thought.'

'What do you mean?' said Amelia.

'Never mind,' said Blanche. 'So, the plot thickens, it seems. I only hope Cynthia has an alibi.'

'Goodness me, will it come to that, do you think?' said Amelia. 'It hadn't occurred to me. But yes, you're right—the police are bound to come back and start asking questions again. They'll want to know where you were at the time of the murder. I wish I'd thought to ask Larry when he died. What time did you get back last night?'

'Oh, lateish. I can't remember exactly when,' said Blanche vaguely.

'Can anyone vouch for that?'

'Probably. I dare say I can find someone.'

'You don't seem to be taking this very seriously, Mummy,' said Amelia. 'Why, don't you realize they might arrest you if you can't prove where you were?'

'Nobody is going to arrest me,' said Blanche. 'I haven't been to Caroline Terrace in weeks, so I couldn't possibly have done it. I expect it was one of the others. I wonder which?'

Amelia said nothing, but darted a worried glance at her mother.

———

IN DOVER STREET, Captain Atherton was sipping tea. His man, Mahomet, stood respectfully to attention.

'Stabbed in the back, eh?' said Atherton. 'Well, there's a turn-up, although I can't say I'm especially surprised. I suppose the police will be all over his house again, now.'

'They will find nothing,' said Mahomet. 'I am certain of that.'

'That's something, at least. Still, I wish we could put an end to this business once and for all. It's damned inconvenient.'

'Indeed, sir,' said Mahomet. 'Is there anything you would wish me to do?'

'I don't see what you can do. The letters have disappeared—presumably hidden somewhere. Unless you have any ideas as to where they might be, all we can do is to wait and hope they never turn up.'

'There is no reason to think they will,' said Mahomet. 'It is unlikely that Weaver had time to make arrangements to pass them on to anybody else, since he died so soon after his employer.'

Something in the tone of his voice caused Captain Atherton to lift his head.

'I dare say you're right,' he said. Then he went on casually, 'I don't suppose you know anything about it, do you?'

'No, sir,' said Mahomet. 'I have no idea who did it.'

Atherton was not looking at his servant at that moment, but if he had been, he might have seen his own curiosity reflected in Mahomet's eyes. After a moment the man begged leave and left the room, and Captain Atherton was left to drink his tea.

―――――

'WHY DIDN'T YOU tell me you knew?' said Lady Bendish to her son. Her eyes were large and dark, and filled with despair.

'How could I?' said Larry Bendish. 'I thought about it occasionally, but I always lost my nerve before I got to the point. And besides, it seemed to me that it was much better not to say a word. I didn't want things to change, you see. And this changes everything.'

'How long have you known?'

'Since I was eight.'

'What?' exclaimed Lady Bendish in horror. 'How can this be?'

He looked uncomfortable.

'I didn't mean to,' he said. 'I promise you I didn't. But you dropped a letter once—I remember, it was shortly after Father died—and I picked it up. I didn't mean to read it, but I saw one or two words that caught my attention, and before I knew it I'd read the whole thing. Of course, I was too young to understand properly at the time, so I kept quiet about it. But when I got older, I realized that we'd both be in trouble if anyone found out. You know how Father's family hate us. They tried their best to overturn his will, and prove that he hadn't been in his right mind when he married you. Of course they failed. He wasn't a young man, but there was nothing wrong with his brain. But I can just imagine how they'd lick their lips if they found this out. They'd have you thrown out on the street before you could say "knife."'

'Your father was an excellent man,' murmured Lady Bendish sadly. 'I only wish he had lived to see you grow up.'

'I hated what they said about you,' said Larry fiercely. 'They were always insinuating things, as though you'd somehow hypnotized him into marriage—as though you were only interested in him for his fame.'

'Well, I certainly didn't marry him for his money, since he gave most of it away,' said Lady Bendish. 'He was always so terribly generous. I loved him for it, of course, but I do wish he'd provided a little better for you.'

'He provided perfectly well for me,' said Larry. 'I have nothing to complain about, and nor does Ann.'

'But what now?' said Lady Bendish. 'As it seems you know, none of it is rightfully ours, anyway. Because of what I am.'

Her tone was bitter.

'You're my dear, sweet mother,' said Larry, 'and I won't let anyone say differently.'

'But the law doesn't care how dear or sweet I am,' she said. 'I wasn't legally married to your father and that's all there is to it.'

'You acted in good faith. You thought your first husband was dead.'

'I did,' she said. 'Everybody did. He disappeared for years, and I thought myself free to marry again. But when I found out he was still alive your father was already dead, so it was impossible to put things right. Then Eduardo died too, and I thought I was safe, since we'd married in Argentina. I thought nobody in England would ever find out.'

'But Ticky did, didn't he?'

Lady Bendish lowered her eyes.

'Yes,' she said.

'How much did he get out of you?'

She waved a hand in a gesture of what might have been desperation.

'I don't know, I never counted. I just paid him whatever he asked. Anything to make him go away. But it wasn't so much the money—I'd have paid him it gladly in return for his silence. It was the taunts I couldn't stand—the constant mocking. I don't believe the money meant a thing to him. I think he just enjoyed having power over people. He took pleasure in the knowledge that his position in society was all thanks to the misery of others.'

'Then he deserved everything he got,' said Larry. 'Good riddance to the man. And to his contemptible servant, too. They're both out of the way now, and you don't have to worry about them any more. I only wish you'd confided in me sooner.'

'Why? What could you have done?'

'I don't know. But I should have thought of something. The man was nothing but a foul parasite—a blood-sucker, feasting on others' misfortune. People of that sort don't deserve to live.'

He sounded so furious that Lady Bendish regarded him in alarm.

'You are just talking out of anger, aren't you, darling?' she said. 'I mean, you didn't—you didn't actually do anything?'

'No, but I wish I had,' said Larry, setting his jaw. 'I should like to find whoever did it and shake him by the hand.'

She gave a little bleat of protest.

'Well, what of it?' he demanded. 'He's done you the most enormous good turn.'

'I wish I could believe it,' she said. 'But the police are no doubt searching the house at this moment, and I'm frightened of what they will find.'

'I don't believe they'll find anything,' said Larry. 'I think Ticky was far too wily to leave anything compromising lying around the house. I expect it's well hidden. And with any luck it will never turn up.'

'I do hope you're right,' she said.

DENIS BEASLEY WINCED as the door slammed behind his wife, then turned to Ann Chadwick.

'I don't seem to be able to say anything to her at the moment,' he said. 'Every time I try to start a perfectly normal conversation she flies off the handle. What was it this time? I only said I suppose we can expect another visit from the police now.'

'I think this whole thing has made her nervous,' said Ann. 'She doesn't like to be reminded of it.'

'Well, there's no need for her to take it out on me,' said Denis. 'And why is she nervous? Don't tell me Ticky had got to her too. Good Lord—that's it, isn't it? He was blackmailing her. What was it? The cocaine, I suppose. I'm sure she thinks I don't know about it, but I'm not stupid. It was perfectly obvious what she was doing.'

'I have no idea,' said Ann untruthfully. 'She's never said anything to me, and I've no reason to suppose she was one of his victims.'

'And you wouldn't tell me even if you did know, would you? You can keep a secret. That's why I tell you all mine. I don't mind you knowing everything about me because I'm certain I can trust you. But one never knows what you're thinking. What are *your* secrets, Ann? You must have some of your own, surely?'

Ann smiled, but said nothing.

'No, you won't give them away,' he said. 'Ticky would have had a hard time of it to find something on you.'

He walked over to the window and looked out.

'There she goes,' he said. 'I expect we won't see her until this evening now, and I'll be at a loose end for the rest of the day.'

'Why don't you go to your club?' suggested Ann.

'I'm too restless with all this murder business. I'll pace up and down and all the old boys will glare at me. I'd be better off going for walk. Will you come with me?'

'No, thank you. I have some letters to write. You go.'

Denis regarded her in silence for a moment as she prepared her writing things.

'I wish I'd kept well away from Natalia,' he said at last. 'I ended things with her after Nancy threatened me with divorce, but I was bored with her anyway.' He paused. 'You know I only took up with her again to make you jealous, don't you?'

'Hush,' said Ann. 'There's no sense in talking like that.'

'And then Maltravers found out about her and started demanding money,' said Denis, ignoring her. 'I'd have told him to go to the devil had it not been for you, but Nancy would have thrown me out, and then I'd never have seen you again.'

Ann glanced at him but said nothing.

'You know how I feel about you, Ann,' he said quietly. 'Won't you say yes? It would make me so terribly happy.'

'How can I?' she said. 'You're married to Nancy. And you seem to forget I'm marrying Larry.'

'Larry doesn't care for you as much as I do,' said Denis.

'Yes, he does—and more so.'

'Do you love him?'

'Of course I do,' she said, without looking at him.

'A bird in the hand, eh?'

'Your words, not mine,' she said sharply. 'But I won't be your plaything. I have too much respect for myself.'

'That's true enough. But if you think I'm playing games with you, you're very wrong. It's not like that. You may not believe me, but my intentions are entirely honourable and above the board. I'd like you to be my wife. I'd see to it you weren't cited in the divorce.'

'I don't want you to divorce Nancy,' said Ann. 'That won't do at all. And I don't think you quite realize what you'd be giving up if you did get divorced.'

'Because she's the one with the money, you mean? I don't care about that any more. They've dangled their wealth in front of me all these years—her father did, anyway—and threatened me with penury if I didn't behave myself. But what sort of a feeble wretch must I have been, to have allowed myself to become a slave to my wife in that fashion? I'm disgusted at myself, and I won't stand for it any more. I don't want her money, and I don't want her. I want to be free again.'

'If you think that by divorcing her you'll win me you're very wrong,' said Ann. 'I won't be associated with anything of the sort.'

'You're right, of course,' he said. 'I can't ask you to be a party to that kind of scandal. And why should you want to marry a middle-aged divorcé with no money and no prospects? You deserve more than that. You oughtn't to be a poor man's wife.' He began pacing restlessly about the room. 'If only things had been different,' he said suddenly. 'If only I weren't already married.'

'But you are,' said Ann.

'If I could snap my fingers now and somehow make Nancy disappear, believe me, I'd do it. I only wish there were a way.'

'Things are never as easy as all that,' she said.

'No,' he said. 'But I shall find a way somehow. I must have you. I've never felt like this before. It's something quite new to me. Of course, you know I've misbehaved in the past, but none of it meant anything. If only you'll say yes, I'll be a perfect angel from now on.'

'Perhaps you ought to be saying that to your wife,' said Ann.

He opened his mouth to speak, but she went over and put a gentle hand to his cheek. He took it and kissed it, then held it in his.

'You've been cooped up indoors too long,' she said after a moment. 'Go for a walk. You'll feel better for it, I promise. And now I really must get on.'

She freed her hand, then sat down at the writing-desk and turned her back to him.

'I see—you're giving me my dismissal, are you?' he said. 'Very well, I'll leave you to it for now, but don't forget what I said. Once this is all over I shall ask you again, and this time you'd better say yes, because I won't take no for an answer.'

So saying, he went out. After the door had closed, Ann let out a little sigh of relief and shook her head. Then she bent to her task, the merest hint of a smile on her face.

CHAPTER SIXTEEN

FREDDY HAD HEARD all about Weaver's murder, of course, but after his adventure with the flask he had judged it best to give the police a wide berth for a little while, just until he could be sure that they had fallen for Bert Evans's story, and were not about to haul up Bert, himself and Cynthia on a charge of tampering with the evidence. So it was that his fellow-reporter Jolliffe was given the job of reporting on this latest development in the Maltravers case for the *Clarion*, while Freddy accepted a lesser story about a collision on Shaftesbury Avenue between an omnibus and a wagon carrying several hundredweight of turnips. When he returned to Fleet Street, he found a scrawled message on his desk to the effect that a Miss Sang Jackamo had been asking for him, and would wait for him at the Lyons until two o'clock. Freddy glanced at his watch and saw that it was nearly ten minutes to, and so with a hurried excuse he ran out again, promising to be back in time to hand in his piece for the early evening edition.

Valentina Sangiacomo was sitting at a corner table by herself, eating a large slice of cream cake with great relish. She nodded as Freddy came in, and pointed at the seat opposite her, then proceeded to polish off the rest of the cake with great efficiency.

'Don't they feed you, these artist chaps?' said Freddy, as she dabbed at her mouth and took a sip of tea.

'Not much,' she said. 'They don't think about that kind of thing. Art before everything else, don't you know? Never mind that the model's starving to death.'

'I can't imagine you ever dying of hunger,' said Freddy. 'You're far too good at taking care of yourself.'

She shot him an amused glance.

'I won't say you're wrong,' she said. 'Aren't you going to have anything?'

'I've already eaten, thanks,' he said, then, as she showed no sign of introducing the matter at hand: 'was this a purely social summons, or do you have something to tell me?'

'What do you think?' she said. 'But I'd like to discuss terms first.'

'Before we do, I think you ought to know something.'

'He's dead. Yes, I know that, of course. Someone stuck a knife in him, and I can't say I blame them, if he really was what you say.'

'You seem to know a lot about it.'

'I can read the papers as well as you can, *Mister* Pilking-ton-Soames,' she said.

'Then presumably whatever you have to tell me occurred on Friday afternoon or Saturday.'

She said nothing, but looked at him expectantly. He sighed, and handed over ten shillings, which she tucked into her dress.

'I hope this is worth it,' he said.

'It's not for me to say.'

'You managed to follow him, then?'

'Yes,' she said. 'On Saturday. All the way to Dorking and back.'

'Dorking? What's in Dorking?'

'His mother, I think,' replied Valentina. 'From what I could see through the window, she looked like him, only a hundred years older and ten times uglier.'

'I see,' said Freddy. The fear was stealing over him that the blackmail business had already been passed on to a third generation of owners. 'So he was visiting his mother like a good boy, yes? Was he—er—carrying anything with him?'

'Not as far as I could tell,' she said. 'He got on the train and sat looking out of the window all the way there, then got off and walked straight to where he was going. It's a little cottage just off the Westcott Road. She keeps chickens and a goat.'

'Did he see you?'

'What do you take me for?' she said. 'I know how to hide myself. Once he'd gone into the house I crept up and peeked through the window. She was all tucked up in blankets and he was serving her tea. I waited, and after a while he came out, so I hid quickly behind the hen-house. I thought he was going to leave, but he only went into the coal-cellar, then back inside. Then it started to get dark, and it was raining a bit, and I thought maybe he was going to stay the night. I didn't much fancy sleeping with the chickens, so I thought I'd go, but then I suddenly remembered the coal-scuttle.'

'Which coal-scuttle?'

'The one by the fire. I saw it when I looked through the window. It was full.'

'So?'

'So why did he go into the coal-cellar?' said Valentina.

'Oh,' said Freddy, in sudden understanding. 'You think he went in for some other reason?'

'Stands to sense, doesn't it?' she said. 'At any rate, that's what I thought, so I sneaked over to have a look inside, but it was locked. A shiny new padlock it was, too. If I'd had something suitable with me I'd have had a go at it, but I didn't.'

'What do you mean, something suitable?'

She looked at him pityingly.

'Good Lord,' he said. 'Don't tell me you're in the habit of carrying a set of lock-picks with you?'

'No,' she said. 'If I was I'd have been able to get in. Anyway, I waited a while longer, and eventually he came out and set off back to the station. I didn't hang about myself, since I couldn't get into the coal-cellar, so I came back to London.'

'That's bad luck about the padlock,' said Freddy regretfully. 'How are we supposed to find out what's in there if we can't get in?'

'Can you pick a lock?' said Valentina.

'It's not the sort of thing they teach at Eton,' said Freddy. 'Pity—it would be much more useful than all that Latin nonsense.'

'I thought you'd say that,' she said. 'Never mind—I can show you how to do it.'

And to his surprise she produced from her pocket a padlock and a metal ring, from which hung a number of odd-looking hooks.

'Ah,' he said. 'So these are what you forgot to take with you on Saturday.'

'Exactly,' she said, and proceeded to show him how to open the padlock. After a few tries Freddy succeeded in doing it himself, much to his excitement. She made him keep practising until he could do it every time, and then gave a satisfied nod.

'You'll do,' she said. 'Now you can get in yourself. I don't fancy going down to Dorking again. It's too countrified for my tastes. Now, what do you say? I reckon that ought to be worth another ten.'

'You're an expensive young woman, Miss Sangiacomo,' said Freddy, as he handed her another note and put the lock-picks in his pocket. 'Tell me, what other services do you offer? Tours of the escape-routes of London? Practical lessons in how to make a useful garotte?'

'There's no need for impudence,' she said without offence.

'Sorry. I'm awfully grateful to you, really I am,' he said. 'Blackmail's a filthy business, and I want to find whatever it is Weaver was keeping before the police get hold of it, and start tramping about, asking awkward questions and causing every-one inconvenience.'

'What'll you do with it if you find it?' she said.

'I haven't quite decided. I suppose one ought to burn it all without reading it, but then the victims won't know they're safe. I may have to send it back to them instead.'

'You don't mind that the murderer won't get caught?' she said curiously.

'I don't know,' he said. 'I mean to say, I'm all in favour of the notion that killing ought to be discouraged in general, but in this case whoever it was seems to have done a number of people a good turn by ridding the world of two individuals who were taking up far too much space in it.'

'Amen to that!' she said, and stood up. 'I'd better be off. Good luck, and don't forget to keep a steady hand.'

'I won't,' he promised, and she went out, leaving him to pay the bill. He watched her leave, and reflected on how many strange and wonderful people there were in London. It seemed to him that she was a very useful person to know, but too late he realized that he did not know how to find her should he ever want to speak to her again. Still, that was not important at present. His main concern now was to get into that coal-cellar in Dorking. But when to do it? He could not go now, as he was wanted at the office. Perhaps it would be better to go this evening—yes, that would be the best idea, since it would be dark, and nobody would see him. He would go alone, in order to avoid attracting too much attention, pick the lock, get whatever it was out of the cellar, and be home by midnight. After that, all would be plain sailing: he would hand over any incriminating information he found to its rightful owners, then let the police go about the business of investigating the murders of Ticky and Weaver without being unduly influenced by motive—for surely there must be enough physical evidence to show who had done it, without their needing to be burdened by the additional knowledge of all the suspects' sins? At any rate, the investigation was now back on course, everything was where it ought to be, and Freddy was feeling more cheerful now than he had for days. He would go back to the office, finish his work, retrieve the information at his leisure, and then stop meddling in the case once and for all.

Chapter Seventeen

'T HERE YOU ARE, Freddy,' said Amelia Drinkwater, jumping up from a chair as he entered through the grand arched doors of the *Clarion* building. 'They said you'd be back soon.'

She was looking very pretty, as usual, and the blue of her eyes was accentuated by the violet coat she was wearing.

'Oh, hallo again,' said Freddy, with a surreptitious attempt at straightening his tie. 'What are you doing here?'

'I've come to find out how you're getting on,' she said.

'Getting on with what?'

'The murder investigation, silly! I suppose you've heard about Weaver. Who did it, do you think?'

'I—' said Freddy, then realized suddenly that since Ticky's death he had given barely any thought to the identity of the culprit, for he had been so busy trying to get himself and his mother out of trouble, and worrying about the information Weaver held and where it might be, that the matter of who had presumably murdered two people had barely raised more than an idle question in his head. 'Why, I don't know,' he said feebly. 'Who do you think it was?'

She gave him a reproachful look.

'Oh, Freddy,' she said. 'I thought you were going to investigate for me. Don't you remember? You agreed to help me, but I don't believe you've done anything at all.'

'Well, I—er—' he said.

'I thought at least you might have spoken to the police to find out whether they have any leads. I mean to say, we can eliminate two people from the investigation at least, which makes things a little easier, but I thought you might have found out something about the other four.'

'Which two people can we eliminate?' said Freddy, surprised.

'Why, your mother and mine, of course! Oh, and Lady Bendish, who's a dear and could never murder anybody. That only leaves three—Captain Atherton and the Beasleys. I don't know about you, but my money's on Captain Atherton. He has a look about him that I don't like, and he probably knows about all kinds of exotic poisons from his time in the jungle.'

'Ticky was killed with nicotine,' said Freddy. 'One can buy that perfectly easily here in London. All one has to do is sign the poison-book.'

'Still, though,' she said. 'I'll bet he's the murderer. I expect all those years abroad warped his brain, and he went mad and started killing people.'

'Do you have any evidence of this?' said Freddy.

'You were supposed to be looking for that,' she said. 'But you don't seem to have done much at all.'

'As a matter of fact, I did find a clue,' he said, 'but I haven't had a chance to pursue it yet.'

'Oh, what is it?' she said excitedly.

'There's a possibility that Weaver hid some documents at a house in Dorking. I thought I might go down there this evening and see if I can retrieve them.'

'What kind of documents? Is it that thing you were talking about? The blackmail, I mean? Is it a file of everybody's secrets? I'll come with you. What time are we going?'

'I was going to go by myself,' he said hastily. 'After all, I don't absolutely know it's there, and it'll be dark, and the more of us there are, the more likely it is that we'll get caught.'

'Nonsense. I can creep just as quietly as you. More quietly, I dare say. Are you really going to break into the house?'

'No, just the coal-cellar,' he said. 'Listen, I'd really rather you stayed here. It's not safe for you.'

'You're wasting your breath,' she said. 'I shouldn't dream of letting you leave me out of an adventure like this, so I'm coming whether you like it or not. Besides, you'll need someone to keep a look-out.'

'Well, I suppose—' he said. Amelia was not the ideal companion for a night excursion of this sort, since she was somewhat excitable, with a tendency to squeal, and he was worried she would give them away. But she seemed so terribly keen to solve the murder—even if her deductive abilities left something to be desired—that he did not feel able to say no. 'Very well, then. But you must promise to keep quiet, because if we're caught we'll get into all kinds of trouble.'

'Of course I shall,' she said.

'Then I suggest we set off at about eight o'clock,' he said. 'It will be fully dark by then, so there's less chance of us being seen.'

She gave him a beaming smile and clapped her hands together.

'How thrilling!' she said. 'All right. I'll see you at Victoria at eight. Don't be late!'

And she went off, leaving Freddy wondering whether he were making a terrible mistake. There was no going back on it now, however, and when he arrived at Victoria at the appointed time to find her already there waiting for him, he was pleased to see that she had had the sense to change into a dark coat and hat, and had adopted a suitably sober expression to match. On the train down to Dorking they were careful not to draw too much attention to themselves. They found an empty carriage, and Freddy explained in a few words what Valentina Sangiacomo had told him, although he judged it better not to mention where he had got the information.

'So you think this notebook, or folder, or whatever it is, might be in the coal-cellar?' said Amelia.

'It's possible. I certainly think it's worth a look. Now, as far as I know, the only person living at the house is Weaver's mother, but we'll have to keep a sharp look-out, just in case.'

'Oh, I forgot to bring a torch,' she said suddenly.

'I have one,' he said, showing her.

'But if the coal-cellar is locked, how are you going to get in?'

'Ah, yes, that's another thing,' he said. 'I hope you don't mind, but I shall have to pick the lock.'

'Can you pick locks?' she said, impressed.

'Oh, yes,' he said modestly. 'It's a little trick I picked up on my travels, from a notorious safe-cracker. You've read about "Fingers" McDougal, I take it? He and I were pretty thick, at one time, before his arrest. He taught me all he knew about getting through locked doors and suchlike, and was rather flattering about my abilities. I'm quite an expert now, although of course I'd never dream of employing my knowledge for anything dishonest.'

'Goodness!' said Amelia, staring. 'Fingers McDougal? What a funny name! Was he called Fingers because he was a thief?'

'Not exactly,' said Freddy. 'He got the name when he had an unfortunate accident with some explosives while trying to break into a bank safe a few years ago. His name ought to have been Thumbs, really, since that's all he was left with. He battled on bravely for a while, but in the end it rather finished his career.'

They had now arrived at Dorking, and alighted from the train.

'My informant says it's just off the Westcott Road,' said Freddy. 'We shall have to walk, I'm afraid, as it's too risky to take a taxi, but it's not much more than a mile or so.'

They set off down the street, and were soon walking out of the town along a dark, quiet road that was lit only by a sliver of a moon. No-one else was about, and all that could be heard was the sound of their footsteps. As they walked, Amelia grasped Freddy's arm.

'You're not frightened, are you?' he said.

'No,' she said stoutly. 'But I don't want to lose you in the darkness.'

'No fear of that,' he said. 'Now, there ought to be a turn-off just along here. Ah! Here we are. Now, we must be very quiet, as we don't want to be heard.'

They had turned onto a narrow lane, which as far as they could see was bounded by tall hedges. The ground underneath them was mostly dried mud, although some patches were still soft from the recent rain, and Freddy switched on his torch, in order that they might not tread in the dirt. At length, they spied a faint light ahead of them. It came from a window, and as they drew closer they could see the dark shape of a little house at the end of the road. Soon they came to an open gate, from which they could just discern a short path leading up to the house. Amelia was now gripping Freddy's arm very tightly, and he extricated himself with care and took her hand, and they tiptoed up to the window, keeping to the shadows as they did so. Freddy peered inside. Through the window he could see a small kitchen that was shabby but homely. A fire burned brightly in the grate, and by it sat an old woman, dressed in rusty black and wrapped in a shawl, reading a Bible. Her finger moved along the lines, and her lips moved as she read. Every so often, she stopped to dab a handkerchief to her eyes. Presumably the police had already broken the news of Weaver's death to her. As Freddy watched, another woman came in. This one was also old, but obviously much less frail, for she immediately started to bustle about the kitchen. There was a resemblance between the two, and Freddy wondered whether they were sisters. The second woman said something to the first, then picked up a blackened kettle and walked towards the door. There was the sound of a key turning in the lock.

Freddy immediately pulled Amelia into the shadows, and flattened her and himself against the wall. The woman came out and walked off into the darkness, seemingly without need of a light. After a minute or two they heard the sound of water being drawn from a pump. Then she came back into the house and shut the door. Freddy breathed a sigh of relief.

'You can let go of me now,' said Amelia after a moment.

'Sorry,' said Freddy, and did so.

'Where's the coal-cellar?' she said. 'Oughtn't we to look for it?'

'Yes,' said Freddy. He glanced along the wall of the house as far as he could see by the light cast through the window. There was no sign of anything that looked like a coal-cellar.

'Perhaps it's around the side,' suggested Amelia. Freddy followed her around the corner of the house. Here, all the windows were in darkness, and the moon had gone behind a cloud, so they could not see a thing. Freddy judged it safe to switch on the torch.

'Look!' whispered Amelia.

Set into the wall of the house was a low, wooden door about four feet high. Freddy trained the torch on it, and saw that the door was fastened with a new-looking padlock. This must be what Valentina Sangiacomo had seen. He handed the torch to Amelia, who pointed it at the door, then crouched down to examine the lock.

'This won't take long,' he said. He took the lock-picks from his pocket and set to work. Alas for all his confidence! For he soon discovered that it was one thing to pick a lock in broad daylight with an instructor to guide him, and quite another to do it on a cold night, in the dark, with a pretty girl gazing at him admiringly. No matter how much care he took to follow Valentina's instructions exactly, and no matter how delicately he prodded and poked at the lock, it refused to yield.

'Is there something wrong with the lock-pick?' said Amelia, after a few minutes in which he had had to bite his lip several times to stop himself from swearing.

'No,' said Freddy, and tried again.

'Perhaps it's a particularly difficult lock,' she said kindly, after another interval. 'I expect he had it made specially to stop burglars.'

Freddy counted to ten under his breath, then sat back on his heels.

'It's no good,' he said. 'I can't open it.'

'Can I help?' said Amelia. 'Perhaps it's a matter of getting the angle right.'

'I've tried every angle on the protractor,' he said, with a slight note of testiness in his voice. 'I don't know why it won't open.'

She took the lock-picks from him and crouched down next to him.

'Here,' she said, and handed him the torch. 'Now, what do I do? I push this one in and wiggle it a bit. Then what?'

'Keep prodding with the other one until you've pushed all the pins back,' said Freddy. 'But it's no good, you won't—'

There was a click, and Amelia let out a little squeal of triumph as she pulled the padlock open.

'Oh, it's *much* easier than it looks, isn't it?' she said. 'You can go in now. I'll wait here and sound the alarm if anyone comes.'

Several remarks went through Freddy's head, but since there was no time to be lost he gave it up and opened the door. Inside was a short flight of steps leading downward, and he cautiously descended. The room was little more than five feet square and the same in height, so he could not stand up straight. A heap of loose coal took up about half the floor, while most of the rest was occupied by various odds and ends such as leaky pails and sticks of old furniture. He was just about to start looking around properly, when he noticed that his torch was fading fast, and this realization had no sooner come to him than it went out altogether.

'Damn!' he said, more loudly than he had intended.

'What's happened?' came a whisper from Amelia through the door. 'Why have you switched the torch off?'

'The battery's gone,' he said.

'Oh, dear,' she said. 'How are you going to find anything in the dark?'

Freddy did not answer, but stretched out his hands carefully. The cellar was so small that from where he stood he could touch the wall on each side. He had not had more than a moment in which to take in its contents before the torch went out, but he was almost sure he had caught a glimpse of a wooden shelf attached to the far wall. His impression was confirmed when he took a cautious step forward, still stooping, and hit his forehead against it. He let out a muffled 'Ouch!' through gritted teeth, and paused for a few moments with his hands to his head. Once his eyes had stopped watering, he reached up carefully and felt for the shelf. After a few moments, his hand encountered something that felt like a bundle of papers wrapped in oilskin, and his heart leapt. This must be it, surely! He picked it up and turned quickly towards the door, but in his haste his foot caught in some object on the floor. He reached out instinctively to put his hand against the wall and thus regain his balance, but missed, twirled, flailed and went over backwards with a deafening crash. From the sound of it, it seemed as though he had succeeded in hitting every object in the cellar on his way down, and had knocked them all against one another too, just to make quite certain that the noise was as loud as it could possibly be. He was now lying sprawled on a heap of coal, without the bundle in his hand. There was no time to be lost. He must find it again, before someone in the house came out to find out what the racket was. He crawled about on the floor, feeling for the thing he had dropped, and finally found it under a broken stool. Then he tucked it inside his jacket and emerged from the cellar, to find Amelia standing there, her hand over her mouth and her eyes wide.

'What happened? Have you got it?' she whispered urgently.

'Yes, I think so,' he said. 'Quick, we'd better get away before they come out and see us.'

But it was too late, for as they rounded the corner of the house they saw the front door open and the second of the two old women come out with a broom.

'Who goes there?' she called, and headed towards them. 'Thieves! Robbers! I warn you, my son is in the house and he's fetching his gun. We'll have the law on you!'

They shrank back into the shadows, Amelia clutching Freddy's arm again. The woman had now switched on a torch and was sweeping it back and forth, looking for the intruders. The claim about her son was surely a lie, but that did not matter, for she did not herself look like a woman who was to be lightly crossed. She approached slowly, and they backed away and looked for a means of escape, but all they could see in the darkness was a hen-house, with behind it a high hedge. Before they could do anything it was too late.

'Aha! There you are!' said the woman, as the light fell on them and they squinted. 'I'll have the police on you, I will. I won't stand for thieves on my property, taking what's ours. Why, you ought—oh!'

Her voice faltered, as she took in their appearance and it dawned upon her that she was not addressing a petty thief, come to steal her chickens, but rather an obviously well-to-do young lady and gentleman, who were creeping around in her garden in the dark for reasons best known to themselves. The woman swiftly reached her own conclusions as to what those reasons were, and drew herself up.

'Well!' she exclaimed. 'What's going on here? Why, you're no better than the rest of us, after all. You oughter think more of yourself, young lady, if you don't want to get into trouble. And as for you,' she went on, addressing Freddy. 'What kind of a gentleman are you, to take a girl into a coal-house? You oughter be proper ashamed of yourself, you ought. I've a good mind to tell your parents what you've been getting up to. Now, go on, get out! Before I'm as good as my word.'

As she spoke, she aimed a swipe at Freddy's head with her broom, which he just managed to dodge, while Amelia gave a

little scream. The two of them needed no further encouragement. Keeping their eyes on the broom, they skirted carefully
around the old woman and ran for the gate. They did not stop
until they reached the Westcott Road, when they slowed down
to catch their breath.

'Oh, goodness!' exclaimed Amelia. 'I was sure she was going
to call the police!'

'I'm not certain she won't change her mind, so it's probably
best we get back to London as quickly as we can,' said Freddy.

They arrived at the station just as the train was about to
depart, and had to run to catch it. Once they had found an
empty carriage, they threw themselves down into their seats.
Amelia was about to say something, but at that moment got
a good look at Freddy for the first time, and began to laugh
very hard.

'What is it?' said Freddy.

'You look as though you've been up a chimney,' she managed
at last.

Freddy glanced down at himself, and found that he was
black with coal-dust from head to toe. He gave an exclamation
and did his best to clean himself up, but with only moderate
success, for there was more coal-dust on him than one handkerchief could easily remove. After a few minutes, Amelia
stopped laughing long enough to help him, and by the time
they arrived in London, he was almost—although not quite—
fit to be seen. It was now nearly midnight, and too late to start
examining the thing they had retrieved from the coal-cellar,

and so they parted, Amelia with many instructions and threats as to what punishments she would inflict upon him if he looked at the documents without her. He made a vague promise, and then went home, clutching the precious package and hoping there might be a little hot water left to allow him to have a bath.

CHAPTER EIGHTEEN

IT WAS TUESDAY morning, and Inspector Entwistle and Sergeant Bird were putting their heads together in Entwistle's office at Scotland Yard.

'Any luck on finding out where the knife came from?' said Entwistle.

'Not yet, sir,' said Bird. 'It's a common or garden kitchen knife of the sort you might buy in any shop in London. It almost certainly didn't belong to Maltravers, though—he had his own matching set, and a pretty swanky one it was too.'

'Then presumably the murderer came prepared,' said Entwistle. 'That speaks of premeditation. He didn't just turn up, lose his temper and strike in anger.'

'Doesn't look like it,' said Bird.

'And Johnson is still trying to trace where the nicotine was bought. That might easily take weeks—if it's possible to trace it at all, in fact, since it's the sort of thing anyone might have at home.'

'It's a bit of a slim hope,' agreed the sergeant. 'Still, we'll keep him on visiting every chemist's shop in the area. There's just a chance that our murderer was careless and bought the stuff quite openly.'

'Very well,' said Entwistle. 'Now, as to alibis for Saturday night between about ten o'clock and one o'clock; I see that Captain Atherton was at home, working on his memoirs. His manservant attests to that, as does his housekeeper. What about Mrs. Van Leeuwen? Have you spoken to her?'

'She was out with friends,' said the sergeant. 'She seemed to have trouble remembering their names at first, but once I'd suggested politely that her memory might improve if she and her solicitor came along to the station, she decided she'd better produce the goods.'

'And these friends confirm her alibi?'

'Yes,' said Bird, looking at his notes. 'She was out with them until two. Next one is Mrs. Pilkington-Soames, who was out in Richmond with her husband and an old friend of his. They both back her up, as you'd expect.'

'Hmm. She's another one. I can't put my finger on it, but I'm sure she's hiding something,' said Entwistle.

'Yes,' agreed Bird. 'Queer that almost as soon as we turned up to search her house for the brandy flask, the taxi-driver conveniently found it for us, don't you think?'

'Think he was lying about it?'

'He was very insistent that we test it for his finger-prints when he brought it in, to prove he'd never touched it,' said Bird. 'That might be suspicious, or it might not.'

'What do you think happened?' said Entwistle.

'I can make a good guess,' said the sergeant. 'Young Pilking-ton-Soames was at Eaton Terrace when we arrived, wasn't he? And he seemed very keen to go and talk to Bert Evans about the flask. I shouldn't be a bit surprised if she had it all along, and he took it and planted it in the taxi, to throw suspicion away from her.'

'You might be right,' said Entwistle. 'I wouldn't put it past him, from what I've seen of him.'

'We can't prove it, though,' said Bird. 'Evans is sticking firmly to his story for now, and swears nobody found the flask for him or told him to bring it in, so there's nothing doing there.'

'And then there's the fact that the body was moved,' said Entwistle thoughtfully. 'Mrs. Pilkington-Soames lived just around the corner from Maltravers, and was the last one to see him alive. It all seems to point to her having done it. She couldn't have moved the body, but she might have got someone else to do it for her.'

'That son of hers again, do you mean, sir? If he did it, we'll have a devil of a job getting it out of him. From what I've seen of him so far he never opens his mouth but to tell a tall story.'

'Press-men,' said Entwistle in disgust. 'They get in the way while we're trying to work, and then print a lot of poppycock that makes the public send us horrified letters about the incom-petence of the police. What about the others?'

'Mrs. Beasley was attending a musical concert held for the benefit of a women's temperance organization, in company with Lady Featherstone,' said the sergeant, 'but she has no alibi as such for the period between ten o'clock and midnight, when she arrived home. Denis Beasley dined at his club, then returned home at eleven. No confirmation of that, since he says there was nobody in the house when he got back. Lady Bendish was visiting a friend in the early part of the evening, but was back by half past nine, she says. Her son was out with his girl until ten, and confirms that his mother was at home when he arrived back.'

'So, four of them have alibis of sorts, and two of them don't. We shall have to look into it further,' said Entwistle. 'I shouldn't be surprised if the four that do have an alibi are lying about it. And nobody on Caroline Terrace has reported seeing anybody wandering about in the street late that night?'

'No such luck,' said Bird.

'Still, I think we can safely assume that whoever killed Weaver must have got into the house by knocking at the door. He let them in, they went into the sitting-room, then he turned away and got a knife in the back.'

'Any further forward on the blackmail theory, sir?' said Bird. 'Have you heard anything from the clippings bureau?'

'I was just coming to that,' said the inspector, extracting several sheets of a letter from an envelope. 'They replied this morning. Nicholas Maltravers was a long-standing client of theirs, and they sent him cuttings regularly. They had a long list of names to look out for, and he'd also instructed them to send him anything that hinted at a society scandal. Here's the list. There are about two hundred people on it. Recognize anyone we know?'

The sergeant took the proffered list and glanced down the page. He whistled.

'That's all of them, isn't it?' he said. 'Atherton—Beasley—Beasley—Bendish. They're all there. Do we know whether the bureau sent Maltravers anything about them? I don't suppose they keep copies of the clippings they send?'

'Not as a rule, unfortunately,' said the inspector. 'They keep a reference of where the article came from, with the date and a short description.'

He handed Bird another sheet of paper.

'"A delightful evening-party,"' read Bird. '"Bankruptcy notices." "Death of a cattle-farmer in Argentina." "A day at the races." "A strange occurrence in Austria." Presumably various people had good reason to want all these things kept a secret.'

'Presumably,' said the inspector. 'They did happen to have duplicates of a few of the clippings they sent. Most of them aren't of any interest to us, but look at this.'

The sergeant took it.

'"Our correspondent understands that a well-known society lady, Mrs. B, was recently arrested and then released without charge, after apparently having been discovered almost unconscious, and in a state of intoxication, outside a fashionable restaurant in Mayfair. It is not the first time the lady in question has had trouble of this sort, for a similar incident occurred a little over a year ago, in a different part of London."'

Bird looked up.

'Mrs. Beasley, do you think?' he said. 'Not something she'd want put about if it is, especially if she's caught up with all this women's temperance stuff.'

'Exactly,' said Entwistle. 'Did she tell you anything more about the organization?'

'Only that it's something to do with Mrs. Belcher.'

'Oh, Mrs. Belcher, is it?' said Entwistle. 'In that case, I can certainly see why Mrs. Beasley wouldn't want it getting about that she'd been arrested for being drunk and incapable.'

'I don't suppose there's anything else in among those clippings, sir?'

'Nothing useful, that I can see,' said the inspector. 'But I have hopes of this list of press references. We'll have to put someone on to looking them all up. Some of them aren't even English newspapers, so it's going to take some time.'

'And even then they might not tell us anything if they're all like this one—"Mrs. B." this, and "Mr. A." that,' said Bird. 'It might take weeks to find out what they all refer to.'

'True enough. Still, if the information doesn't help us solve the crime, it might at least be useful for evidence if it comes to a trial.'

'*If* it comes to a trial,' repeated the sergeant.

'It will,' said Entwistle. 'Set the men on to checking those alibis. We must keep trying. There were only six of them there at Babcock's, and one of them has murdered twice. If only they'd be a bit more helpful. Why, none of them seem to care in the slightest about finding the killer.'

'But why should they, if Maltravers was blackmailing them? They're probably only too pleased he's dead.'

'It's pure arrogance, that's what it is,' said Entwistle. 'They're all rich and well-connected, and they think nobody can touch them. Well, they're wrong. I'm going to find out who killed Nicholas Maltravers and arrest them if it's the last thing I do.'

Chapter Nineteen

L ATER THE SAME day Freddy and Amelia met for lunch, and to examine their prize.

'Do you swear you haven't looked at it?' said Amelia, as Freddy placed the parcel on the table between them.

'I only glanced at it for a second, to make quite certain we have the right thing,' he said. 'It wouldn't look too good if we'd stolen Mrs. Weaver's gilt-edged stock certificates and deprived her of her livelihood, would it?'

'And do we? Have the right thing, I mean.'

'I should say so,' he said grimly. He unwrapped the oilskin parcel, inside which was a large envelope. He opened it, took out its contents and glanced through them, handing them to her one by one. There were papers, letters, newspaper-clippings, a card with a pressed flower on it, smelling faintly of perfume, and even a woman's gold ring. Amelia took the ring and tried it on.

'Whose is this, I wonder?' she said. 'And why was Ticky keeping it?'

'Presumably because it incriminated someone,' said Freddy. 'My word! It looks as though he'd been running his blackmail business for years. Here's something from nineteen sixteen. It seems someone lied about his war record, and Ticky caught him at it and made him pay.'

He handed a letter to Amelia, and she read it with a look of distaste on her face.

'This is rather horrid,' she said at last. 'I don't know that I like prying into people's secrets. Can't we just burn it all instead, and pretend we never saw it?'

'I don't think we can,' he said. 'If we do, then the victims won't know they've nothing to worry about any more.'

'But why did they keep paying? Why on earth wasn't he stopped sooner?'

'I expect because people were too frightened to speak up,' said Freddy. 'He'd wormed his way into society and set himself up nicely in position, and once he was there it was difficult to dislodge him without all sorts of unpleasantness coming out.'

'Well, I know it's not the done thing to say it, but I'm glad he's dead,' said Amelia. 'And I'm glad, too, that someone stopped Weaver before he had a chance to make even more people miserable.'

'Yes,' said Freddy. 'His foray into the business didn't last long, did it? That will teach him to be so insufferably pleased with himself. He was certain that he wouldn't be taken the way Ticky was, but he was wrong. After all, it's all very well to be careful, but if one's livelihood depends on meeting one's victims in person to collect the cash—well, then, one jolly well ought to look out.'

He returned his attention to the sheaf of papers. He was unwillingly impressed at Ticky's methodical approach to black-mail, for to each document was appended a sort of statement of account, which listed, in shorthand, the name of the victim in question, his or her presumed transgression, and a tally of monies received. In a separate section Ticky had jotted down notes, some of which were too cryptic to understand, although others were clear enough. 'Threatened to break my legs. Rate to increase from next month,' said one note. 'Wept and said would confess all to husband—dissuaded,' said another. Freddy was conscious of a feeling of disgust as he leafed through the papers. How much misery was contained therein! How many people had sinned and suffered for it at the hands of Ticky Maltravers! At that moment, he began seriously to think that it might be better if the murderer were never found, for surely there was no danger of him killing again, now that the pesti-lence was safely disposed of and there was no further threat?

'Is there anyone we know in there?' said Amelia impatiently. He glanced up.

'Most of these we can put aside,' he said. 'But I've found one or two names I recognize, including my mother's. Oh, don't worry, I know all about it,' he hastened to assure her, as he saw her horrified look. 'She did something rather stupid, that's all. I mean to say, she hasn't committed any crimes or anything. Not that I know of, anyhow,' he added.

He took Cynthia's account, folded it, and put it in his pocket.

'Is there—is there—anything for Mummy?' said Amelia hes-itantly, and his heart melted at her fearful expression.

'Not that I can see,' he said. 'Look for yourself.'

'I—I think I'd rather not,' she said.

There was silence for a few minutes as Freddy continued to turn over the papers.

'Beasley, Denis,' he said at last.

The entry in question was a letter, written in a woman's hand.

'Well, that's hardly a surprise,' said Freddy. 'The usual story,' he went on, in answer to Amelia's inquiring look. 'I expect you can guess. He's well known for it, so I can't think why he put himself in Ticky's power on this occasion.'

He put the paper to one side.

'Beasley, Nancy. Hmm,' he said, but made no further comment. 'Ah! Here's something. Captain Maurice Atherton, your favourite suspect. There are several letters here, and to judge from his statement of account, he paid Ticky rather a lot.'

Amelia said nothing, but he noticed she was starting to look slightly sick.

'Now, what's this?' he went on. 'Lady Bendish. I wonder—'

'Don't!' said Amelia, before he could go on. 'Don't tell me! I don't want to know. How can you look at all these things in such a hard-hearted way? These are all real people, not just entries on a list. Don't you feel any sympathy for them at all?'

Freddy might have pointed out that she had been only too keen on the thing yesterday, but he did not.

'Of course I do,' he said instead. 'It's a foul business. But you forget that one of these people has almost certainly committed murder at least twice. It's tempting to say the dead men deserved it, but that won't matter to the police. They don't care about that.'

Amelia looked down at the table and pushed a spoon about.

'I wish we hadn't started this,' she said at last. 'Can't we leave it?'

'But you said yourself that if we do then the police might never solve the case, and everyone will remain under suspicion.'

'I know what I said. It's just that—now we come to it, I can see it's not as much fun as it was before.'

'No,' he said gently. 'It's not, is it? But I think I ought to keep going, now that I have all this information. I'm not going to give it to the police, but it will be more difficult for them to solve the case without it, and there's a risk they might arrest the wrong person if they don't know all the facts. I think I shall have to do a little digging myself, and then with any luck, if the police do get it all wrong, I shall be able to set them right.'

'Yes, that makes sense,' she said. 'What shall you do now? I mean, with all the evidence.'

'Well, the only documents that matter for our purposes are the ones that pertain to the people who were in Babcock's with Ticky that night. I shall keep those for now, and return the rest to their rightful owners—anonymously, I think, with a note to the effect that their accounts are now fully paid up and no further money is owing.'

'Oh, yes, do,' she said.

'And after that, I think I shall have to go and speak to our lot in person, one at a time—always supposing they don't take me for yet another blackmailer and biff me one on the nose as soon as I turn up.'

'Oh, I do hope they won't!' she exclaimed. 'You've been such a sport about all this that I should hate anything bad to happen to you.'

Her expression was so sweet and sincere that he might have kissed her there and then, but, perhaps fortunately, she was sitting across the table from him, out of reach, and so he had to content himself with a smile. Shortly after that, she announced that she had promised to meet a friend, and left.

Freddy walked slowly back to the *Clarion*'s offices, thinking alternately about Amelia and the work that lay ahead of him, then, once back at his desk, started shuffling papers busily. Anyone looking at him would have thought he was working hard on a story, but in fact he was preparing to draw up a letter to enclose with the various objects and documents that he intended shortly to begin sending back to the victims of Ticky Maltravers. He was leafing through them all, wondering where to start, when a piece of paper detached itself from the pile and floated gently to the floor. He bent to pick it up and was just about to put it back in the envelope when something caught his eye, and caused him to look at it more carefully. It was a cutting from a newspaper, containing a short article and a photograph. It appeared to be from a year or two ago. Freddy pursed his lips in a silent whistle.

'Well, I'll be damned,' he said at last. 'Who would have thought it? But it can't be the same person, surely?'

He peered at the photograph closely, then held it at arm's length and regarded it with his head to one side. Then he spent some minutes hunting about for an accompanying statement of account, but there appeared to be none.

'Impossible to be certain,' he said, looking at the picture once more. 'But it bears further inquiry, I should say.'

'Do stop talking to yourself, Freddy, old chap. I'm trying to concentrate,' said Jolliffe at the next desk.

'Sorry,' said Freddy, and stood up.

'Now where are you going?' said Jolliffe. 'Old Featherstone's coming for his tour of inspection at four, and you'll be in trouble if you're not here.'

'I—er—just need to go and look something up in the archives,' said Freddy. 'I won't be long.'

And off he hurried. He was most likely mistaken in what he had seen, but there was no harm in making sure.

CHAPTER TWENTY

FOR THE NEXT few days, Freddy was taken up with sending back the documents and personal effects he had abstracted from the house in Dorking to their rightful owners. This took no little time, for Ticky's collection had been a large one, and it was not always immediately clear who the owners were. Far more often than he liked, Freddy was forced to read a document and take to himself a secret that another had paid good money to keep hidden, in order to find out who it belonged to, and by the end of the whole thing he felt somehow tainted by the experience, and wanted nothing more than to submerge himself in a hot bath and scrub himself clean of all the unpleasantness.

But there was more to do, for the hardest task still lay ahead of him. He had told Amelia Drinkwater that he did not intend to pass on the information about their friends to Scotland Yard, but without it the police were working partly in the dark, and since he did not wish them to fasten upon the wrong suspect for want of the proper information, he had decided to do a little investigating himself. Furthermore, after a night of wrestling with his conscience, he had reluctantly begun to reach the conclusion that it was only right that the murderer be caught, even though whoever it was had put two loathsome individuals out of the way and, by doing so, saved countless people from further misery. Although Freddy had few qualms about keeping secrets from the police if he considered it necessary, he was not comfortable with the idea of allowing a cold-blooded murderer to get away scot-free—for there was no getting around it: the murders had been carried out deliberately and with premeditation. He did not like the thought of handing over someone who had presumably been unhappy and desperate, but still, he knew it ought to be done.

But how to go about the investigation? He could not simply roll up to each suspect's house and start demanding they produce alibis for the night of Weaver's murder. It was a pity he had rather burned his bridges behind him with regard to the police, for he was certain that his attempts to cover his own and his mother's traces had caused them to suspect him, and he was still by no means confident that they would not, sooner or later, find out the part he had played in getting Cynthia out of trouble. Even if the police had no proof at present, he thought it prudent not to irritate them unduly by turning up and asking questions. It was a pity; Sergeant Bird had seemed a friendly sort, and a useful acquaintance to have, and Freddy wished fervently that he might go and speak to him about various things he wanted to know. But that would be foolish, and so he rejected the idea almost as soon as it entered his head.

Then what ought his next move to be? His first instinct had been to hand all the incriminating documents back to their owners in person—for he certainly did not want to keep them in his possession for longer than necessary—and at the same time question them artfully about the murders. But would they be likely to give anything away to him if they had said nothing to the police? He did not think so.

'What can I say to them?' he said to himself. '"Here are your documents—oh, and by the way, you didn't happen to murder Ticky, did you?" No, that's no good at all.'

Which was the best way to approach the investigation, then? Through pure deduction, perhaps? If he studied the papers carefully enough, might they not point to the culprit? It did not seem likely. As he knew only too well, motive was not proof of anything. What he needed was concrete evidence— someone who had witnessed the poison being put in the flask, for example, or finger-prints on the knife that had been used to kill Weaver. But that sort of thing was the province of the police, and if they still did not know who had done it, then how was he to fare any better?

At the thought of the documents, he remembered his mother. He was fairly certain it was safe to return *her* papers to her, at least. She might be irritatingly obtuse on this par- ticular subject, but he was almost sure she had not murdered anyone—and besides, even if she had, he was not about to give her away to the police, whatever he might be persuaded to do with regard to the rest of them. Accordingly, he took the first opportunity to return the record of Ticky's blackmail to her. Cynthia was delighted when Freddy handed her the sheet of paper on which Ticky had kept a note of the sums she had paid him over the past two years.

'Oh, how simply marvellous, darling!' she said. 'I knew you'd manage it somehow. Now your father need never know a thing about it. Goodness me! Did I really pay him all that money? That's rather a lot, isn't it?'

'I hope this will be a lesson to you,' said Freddy. 'Gambling's a fool's game. You'll never make a profit out of it.'

'Of course you're right,' said Cynthia, 'and I promise you I shall be good from now on. I mean, I know I lost a little the other night, but it was really *only* a little—barely enough even to count as a loss. It's all a matter of knowing when to stop, I see that now.'

There was no use in arguing with her, so Freddy turned the subject to the one that really interested him.

'Listen,' he said. 'I don't suppose you've been thinking much about the murders at all?'

'Which murders?' said Cynthia in surprise.

'Ticky and Weaver,' said Freddy patiently.

'Oh, *those.* No, I can't say I have. Have they found out who did it yet?'

'No. But I was wondering whether you might know.'

'I haven't the faintest idea, darling,' she said. 'Isn't that the police's job?'

'Well, yes,' said Freddy. 'But they don't know about the black-mail—or at least, I don't think they do—and I'm sure you'd rather they never found out. The trouble is that where there's murder involved they'll keep on digging until they unearth something, so if you don't want them to discover what you've been trying to hide, then you'd better hope they arrest someone soon.'

'Oh, but they can't possibly care about my little problem with Ticky, can they?' said Cynthia. 'Why, you've just handed me the evidence he kept. I shall throw it on the fire, and then there'll be nothing at all to worry about.'

'Not for *you*, perhaps. But what about your friends? Didn't you say they were all being blackmailed too?'

'Did I?' she said vaguely. 'Oh, yes, I'd forgotten about that. Still, they're safe now, aren't they? I expect it was all rather a relief to them.'

Freddy opened his mouth to reply, but then he suddenly remembered what it was that had been eluding him.

'Mother,' he said, 'did you see Ticky's present before he was given it? I mean, did you know it was going to be a flask?'

'Why, I don't think I did,' she said. 'I thought Nancy had said she was going to buy him a pocket-watch, but she obviously changed her mind at the last minute. And then of course she left it at home anyway, and Ann had to send Larry in with it.'

Freddy looked at her in astonishment.

'*What*?' he said.

'I said, she left it at home anyway—'

'Yes, I heard you,' he said. 'Why didn't you mention this before?'

'Didn't I? I dare say I forgot. Is it important?'

'It might be,' he said. 'Do the police know?'

'Well, I don't believe I told them,' she said. 'I suppose someone else might have—although I expect most of them didn't notice, since he just came in and handed it to a waiter quickly without stopping at our table, and Ticky and I were the only ones facing the door. They'd been to the theatre, and didn't want to stop. At least, that's what Nancy told me.'

Freddy was thinking very hard. So Larry had also had his hands on the flask, had he? Might he have found the opportunity to tamper with it? He pulled at his nose in irritation. The more he looked into the matter the more complicated it seemed to become.

'Now, listen, Mother,' he said at last, 'I should like you to think very hard, as it might be important. Try and remember: which of the others at Babcock's knew the present was going to be a flask rather than a pocket-watch?'

'Must we really go over this again?' said Cynthia, then, as Freddy looked at her sternly, sighed, and said, 'All right, then, let me think. I'm fairly sure the Van Leeuwen woman didn't know, as she and Captain Atherton were looking at it together, and I seem to recall their agreeing that the flask was a more appropriate choice. Yes—I remember it particularly, because she was taking every opportunity she could to flirt with him and brush her hand against his. Quite brazen, she was, as a matter of fact.'

'Very well,' said Freddy. 'Who was next to Captain Atherton?'

'Nancy. She knew, of course, but I can't remember what she did with the flask. Then it was Sarah Bendish. I've no idea whether she knew, but she certainly didn't think much of it, because she gave it half a glance and then passed it on almost immediately. I wasn't looking at Denis, so I've no idea what he did with it.'

'But presumably he knew it was going to be a flask rather than a watch?'

'Yes, I expect so,' said Cynthia.

'And you don't remember whether you told all this to the police?'

'I may have done,' she said. 'Or did I? One has so many things on one's mind that it's terribly easy to get confused.'

Freddy raised his eyes to heaven.

'Look—' he began, but before he could go on, Cynthia glanced at him and gave him what was meant to be a reassuring smile.

'Look, darling, the police have it all in hand, I'm sure, so I should stop worrying and leave them to it if I were you,' she said.

And with that she went away, leaving Freddy in the usual state of exasperation she tended to provoke in him. Still, she had given him some useful information for once, but what was he to do next? None of it was proof of murder. He was beginning to think that the killer of Ticky and Weaver would never be caught—at least, not if his mother and her friends had anything to do with it, for they had all proved most unwilling to co-operate with the police investigation. It was almost as though they did not *want* the murderer to be found. Of course, he was still struggling with the question himself, and so he could hardly blame them if they preferred to breathe a quiet sigh of relief and pretend the whole thing had never happened. But he was now very curious to identify the culprit, and was determined to do a little more poking about, even if it turned out there was not enough evidence to bring a prosecution. He sat for a few moments, pondering his next move, then decided to pay a visit to the Beasleys.

CHAPTER TWENTY-ONE

DENIS WAS NOT at home when Freddy arrived at Charles Street, but Nancy was there and only too happy to receive him.

'Hallo, Freddy, darling,' she said. 'I haven't seen you in an age. How's Cynthia? I expect you've heard all the news—oh, yes, of course, I saw your piece about Ticky in the *Clarion*. I must say, you did a fine job of puffing him up and pretending he'll be sorely missed.'

'Thank you. It was the least I could do,' said Freddy. 'Hallo, Ann. Nancy's working you hard, I see. I expect you'll be glad to exchange this servitude for a different one once you're married to Larry.'

'Don't be naughty,' said Nancy. 'Ann's very happy here, aren't you, Ann?'

'Perfectly happy, thank you,' said Ann. 'Here's your post. I've sorted it into piles for you. These ones here aren't important, but you'd better have a quick look at these three, and I'll reply to them if you'll just give me a yes or a no. This one's the invitation to Lady Featherstone's Christmas ball.'

'How splendid!' said Nancy, clapping her hands delightedly. 'Success at last! We'll say yes to that one, of course.'

'You're fortunate to have such an efficient helper,' observed Freddy, as Nancy glanced through the other letters. 'Why, you hardly have to do a thing yourself.'

'Oh, it's true! I can't think what I did before she came. When she arrived I was all at sixes and sevens because Father had just died, and I was distraught and couldn't manage everything. But she had everything organized beautifully within two days, didn't you, Ann?'

'Well done,' said Freddy. 'I could do with someone like that myself.'

Nancy was looking at a letter in distaste.

'Ugh!' she exclaimed. 'It's from Aunt Alice. She's threatening to visit next week. She wants to know all about our recent excitement, she says. Why must people be so ghoulish?' She heaved a great sigh. 'What a bore this whole thing is. The police are being tiresome, of course. They're looking at blackmail as a motive now, and they actually asked me to my face whether I had secrets to hide.'

'And do you?' said Freddy.

'Of course I do,' said Nancy. 'But I was hardly going to tell the police that, was I? Then Inspector Entwistle asked whether we keep any nicotine in the house—you know, for gardens and suchlike, so I pointed out that we don't have a garden, and he had to go away. Silly man.'

'He has to do his duty,' said Freddy.

'Well, he needn't bother me while he's doing it,' said Nancy.

'I gather they want to know how the poison got into the flask,' said Freddy.

'Yes. I told them I hadn't the faintest idea. They seem to think one of us did it when it was being passed around the table, but really, that's absurd. To do it in full view of everybody like that! Why, it's nonsensical. It would have been the most awful risk.'

'True, and I don't see why it had to be one of you, either. Lots of people must have handled it before it got to Ticky.'

'I know I did,' said Ann.

'And didn't Larry, too?' said Freddy. 'My mother said he brought it in when you left it at home accidentally.'

'Oh, yes,' said Nancy. 'So silly of me, after all the trouble I went to with it. It's just lucky that Ann and Larry were out at the theatre across the road, and thought to bring it with them.'

'Unlucky for Ticky, though,' said Freddy.

'Well, yes, that's true enough,' admitted Nancy.

'I suppose it was already wrapped when you gave it to Larry?' Freddy said to Ann casually. She was not fooled.

'Are you suggesting he might have tampered with it on his way in?' she said in amusement.

'Not at all, not at all,' said Freddy hurriedly. 'I just meant to say that if it wasn't wrapped, then it goes to show that anyone might have done it. He handed it to a waiter, didn't he? And perhaps the waiter gave it to someone else, who gave it to someone else again. Who knows how many people handled it before it arrived at the table?'

'I couldn't tell you,' said Ann. 'But it was certainly wrapped, although not very tightly. I suppose it's always possible that someone undid the paper and then wrapped it up again afterwards.'

'There's no reason it should have been any of us, or even anybody at Babcock's,' said Nancy. 'It might even have come from the shop. The police ought to be asking at Harrods. I shouldn't be a bit surprised to discover they have a homicidal maniac working there.'

'It would be lucky for you if they did,' said Freddy. 'Although I shouldn't rely on the notion, if I were you.'

'Where is Denis?' said Nancy impatiently. 'He said he'd be back by two, and it's almost four now.'

'There he is,' said Ann, looking out of the window. 'He's just coming now. Oh, and there are the police. I wonder what they want.'

Freddy joined her at the window, and saw Inspector Entwistle and Sergeant Bird getting out of a police-car.

'I say, they're looking rather serious,' he said. 'Perhaps they've found something out.'

Denis stopped to speak to them for a moment, then the three of them turned and entered the house. Soon their footsteps could be heard on the stairs, and Freddy and Ann glanced at one another.

'The police want a word with you, Nancy,' said Denis, as he came into the living-room, followed by Entwistle and Bird.

'Why, of course,' said Nancy politely. 'How may I help you, inspector? I hope you're well.'

But Inspector Entwistle had no time for polite nothings. He was here to do his duty.

'Mrs. Nancy Beasley,' he said, 'I am here to arrest you for the murders of Nicholas Maltravers and James Weaver. I must inform you that anything you say may be taken down and used as evidence.'

'What?' said Nancy in astonishment. 'What on earth are you talking about? I haven't murdered anybody. Tell him, Denis.'

'Er—' said Denis, who seemed as surprised as she.

Inspector Entwistle moved forward to apprehend Mrs. Beasley, and she took a step back.

'Don't be ridiculous,' she said. 'You can't arrest me. Where's the proof?'

'We have information that you purchased a quantity of nicotine from a chemist's shop on Oxford Street on the twenty-seventh of last month,' said Inspector Entwistle.

'What? But I didn't!' exclaimed Nancy. 'I've never bought the stuff in my life. I didn't kill Ticky. And I didn't kill his horrid servant either. Why, I couldn't have! I was out with Lady Featherstone—and let me tell you, I shall very shortly be speaking to her husband, Sir Aldridge Featherstone. He owns the *Clarion*, and I've no doubt he'll be *most* interested to hear the police have been making false accusations all over the place.'

'Lady Featherstone says you left her at ten o'clock that night, but by your own account you didn't arrive home until midnight,' said Inspector Entwistle, unmoved by the threat of publicity.

'Why, I—did she?' said Nancy, taken aback. 'But it was after eleven when we parted, I know it was after eleven. She must have made a mistake. Perhaps her watch was wrong. Go and ask her again. Denis, tell them I didn't do it.'

'Of course you didn't do it,' said Denis. 'Why, I might have done it myself, for that matter—I got back at eleven, but I can't prove it, since nobody was at home. I didn't do it, of course,' he went on hurriedly, 'but just because a person doesn't have an alibi doesn't mean they're guilty of murder.'

'Perhaps,' said Entwistle. 'That will be for a court to decide.'

Nancy gave a little scream.

'A court? It won't come to that, will it? But I swear I didn't do it! Denis!'

She turned appealing eyes to her husband.

'Hush, now,' said Denis. 'The police have got it wrong, that's all. Listen, old girl, it's probably best to go to the station with them now, and answer their questions, while I give Sanderson a call. Don't worry, he'll come along and get you out in no time.'

'I'm not going with them,' said Nancy, who was becoming increasingly agitated. 'You can't make me. I won't be arrested as though I were some sort of criminal. Oh! I'm feeling faint,' she said, and put a hand to her head. She had gone very white and was breathing rapidly.

'I'll get your smelling-salts,' said Ann in concern. 'Where's your handbag?'

She looked about, spotted the little bag on a chair, and hurried to pick it up, but in her haste tipped most of its contents onto the floor.

'Just a moment,' said Inspector Entwistle, placing a firm hand on Ann's arm to hold her back as she bent to retrieve the fallen articles. 'What's this?'

He stooped and picked something up. Even from where Freddy stood at the other side of the room there was no mistaking the little bottle, with the word 'POISON' printed in large letters on its label. Nancy screamed again.

'Oh! What is it?' she cried.

'Nicotine,' said Entwistle, showing Bird the bottle.

'Nancy!' said Denis, as his wife swayed where she stood. 'Quick, give her the salts!'

There was a loud thud. Nancy had fainted.

'Too late!' said Ann, the smelling-salts still in her hand, as the police rushed forward.

CHAPTER TWENTY-TWO

LATER THAT EVENING, once the fuss had died down a little, Freddy went back to his rooms and set himself to think properly about the Ticky Maltravers case. Now that Nancy Beasley had been arrested, it was clear to him that the mystery must be solved, and quickly, lest the wrong person be hanged, for he was almost certain she had not done it, although he could not quite say why. So it was that he brought out his notebook and wrote down everything he knew about the events surrounding Ticky's death, and about the suspects and their motives, and anything else he could think of. After that, he thought about the evening at Babcock's, and what he had been told about it, hoping in this way to eliminate at least some of the suspects.

First there was his mother. Freddy did not spend more than a minute thinking about her, for he would not believe she had done it (moreover, what he would do if it turned out that she *was* the culprit, and that Mrs. Beasley was in real danger of being found guilty in her stead, was something he did not wish to think about at that moment).

Very well, then; leaving Cynthia aside, who was next? Blanche Van Leeuwen had been the first to take the flask when it had been passed around the table. However, it looked as though she could not have put the poison in it, for according to Cynthia she and Captain Atherton had pored over it together. If that were true—and Blanche herself had said something about having watched Atherton while he had the flask—then that let both of them out. Of course, there was always the possibility that the two of them had been in it together, but since Cynthia had been watching them and had noticed nothing suspicious, Freddy could only assume they had not. Furthermore, they had both been expecting the gift to be a pocket-watch. This, although not conclusive evidence, was an important point, for all the signs showed that Ticky's murder had been premeditated, meaning that the killer must have had good reason to believe that he or she would find the opportunity to administer the poison at some time during the evening. But neither of them had known about the flask, and if Blanche in particular were the guilty party, then in that case surely she would have put the poison in his dinner or his wine much earlier, before the gift was presented? After all, she had been sitting next to Ticky and it would have been easy enough for her to do.

The next person to take it had been Nancy, who had, of course, been the one to arrange the purchase. Cynthia had been unable to say what Nancy had done with the flask—but that did not matter, for she had had every opportunity to put the nicotine in it long before they had got to the restaurant. The same was true of Denis Beasley, of course. If either of them were the guilty party, then it made no sense for them to have done it at Babcock's and risk being seen. No; they would have done it at home, naturally, before it was wrapped up. That left Lady Bendish, who, according to Cynthia, had held the flask for only a second or two before passing it on to Denis. It rather looked, therefore, as though she had not had the time to do it either.

On reflection, it seemed to Freddy that the whole theory of someone's having put poison in the flask in a crowded restaurant, in full view of everyone, was fraught with difficulties—not least because half the party had had no idea what the gift was going to be, and so why should they have been carrying around a bottle of nicotine on the off-chance that they would have the opportunity to use it? But if the flask had not been poisoned at Babcock's, then it must have happened either at the Beasleys' house, or on the way to the restaurant. Nancy might well have done it, of course—the police certainly thought so, and the evidence all seemed to point that way, since the nicotine had actually been found in her possession. But set against that was the fact that on the night of this supposedly premeditated murder, she had accidentally left the murder weapon at home, and someone had had to send it in after her. That was an inefficient way of going about things, to say the least, and from what Freddy knew of Nancy, was just like her. Conclusive as the evidence looked, he did not really believe she had the intelligence to plan and carry out such a thing. What about Denis, then? He might easily have done it and planted the poison among his wife's possessions, although Sergeant Bird had told Freddy that the name on the poison-book was Nancy's, which indicated that a woman had made the purchase. But if Denis had gone to all the bother of paying hush-money to Ticky in order to prevent Nancy from divorcing him, then why would he try and pin the blame on her for murder? Presumably because he would then inherit her money if she were hanged. It seemed an unduly complicated way of getting rid of one's wife, but Freddy supposed stranger things had happened.

The only other two people who were known to have handled the flask were Larry and Ann. Ann had bought the thing, of course, and had sent it into Babcock's, whereas Larry had had it in his hand for only a few minutes—and in those few minutes would have had to unwrap it, put the stuff in it, and make up the parcel again somewhere in the street, in full view of the public. But did Larry have a motive? He certainly did if he knew his mother's secret, and the fact that she was being blackmailed for it. He was fond of his mother, and hot-headed enough to have done it if he thought she were in trouble. Freddy wondered whether Larry had an alibi for Weaver's murder—or whether any of them did, in fact.

He glanced at his watch. It was half past nine. He decided to go back to Charles Street and see if he could speak to Denis, under the pretence of offering his support now that Nancy had been taken away by the police. Perhaps he could introduce the subject of alibis without being too obvious about it. But when he got there a servant informed him that Mr. Beasley was at his club, and Miss Chadwick had already retired for the night. Freddy was momentarily surprised that anyone should think of going to bed before midnight, but accepted his dismissal without protest. After hesitating a minute or two on the pavement outside, he decided that since he was out, he might as well pursue Denis to his club and speak to him there.

'Hallo, old chap,' said Denis, when Freddy finally ran him to earth. 'Have you come to help me drown my sorrows? Bring me another, Jarvis, and one for my friend here.'

His face was blotched and his speech was slurred, and he was evidently in drink. The waiter brought whisky, and Freddy sat down and regarded Denis sympathetically.

'How's Nancy?' he said.

Denis shrugged.

'Don't know,' he said. 'The solicitor has been down there, and he says she's doing as well as can be expected. I dare say she'll survive.'

'Have they charged her with murder?'

'Not yet,' said Denis. 'But I expect it's only a matter of time. Funny, isn't it?' he went on. 'Two days ago I was all set to tell her I wanted a divorce, but I can't do that to the old girl now, can I? I mean to say, it would look churlish, to say the least, in the circumstances. Rats deserting a sinking ship, and all that, what?'

'You wanted a divorce?' said Freddy, pricking up his ears. 'On what grounds, if you don't mind my asking? Did you have evidence that she—er—'

Denis shook his head resolutely, as though he wanted to make quite sure it was still attached to his shoulders.

'No. No,' he said firmly. 'She wouldn't do anything like that, I'm certain of it. She's a good girl, my Nancy. Far too good to do that to me, even though she'd have had every right, given the behaviour she's had to put up with from me over the years.

But I've had enough of all that, now. None of them mattered a jot, you know, but what's a man to do when his wife has all the money?'

'Did she lord it over you, then?'

'Not she, so much,' said Denis. 'I'll give her that. She never rubbed it in. But her father, now—he was a different matter altogether. You see, she'd go to him whenever I misbehaved. Can't say I blame her—I was pretty incorrigible, and she always knew he'd be sympathetic and take her part. And did he! The number of times I was summoned to that ghastly old mausoleum of theirs down in Hampshire for a carpeting. He kept her short deliberately—as a kind of punishment to me, I think. He said he wasn't going to give his daughter money only for it to be thrown away on fur coats for whores and chorus-girls. And he was right, too, as that's what I'd have spent it on. But no more. I'm done with that, now—ashamed of it, in fact. Funny how one's life can change in only a few months, isn't it? If you'd told me this time last year that I was about to fall in love and resolve to give up all my old ways, I should have laughed at you. I've never been the sort to lose my head over a woman, but I suppose the madness can strike at any age. Have you ever been in love?'

'Once or twice,' said Freddy.

'Ghastly, isn't it? It makes one do all kinds of things one wouldn't normally dream of doing.'

'Such as asking one's wife for a divorce, do you mean?'

Denis heaved a sigh.

'Well, it's too late for all that. It's just lucky she never agreed to anything, because I can't go through with it now.' He regarded the contents of his glass and nodded slowly, with the air of a man thinking profound thoughts. 'I must be fonder of the old girl than I thought,' he said. 'I should never have believed it of myself, but I'm rather worried about what might happen to her now the police have got their hands on her. Stupid of me, what?'

'She's your wife,' said Freddy. 'Of course you're worried.'

'And yet only the other day I was saying that if I could snap my fingers and have her disappear, I'd do it. But I never dreamt anything like this would happen. That's not what I wanted at all. I didn't want her hurt; I just wanted her—I don't know—gone, I suppose. I can't have her, can I?' he said suddenly. 'I promised her the earth, but it can't be done. I must stand by the wife I have. It's the right thing to do. It was idiotic of me ever to think I could start afresh and pretend the past had never happened. The law and society don't look kindly upon that sort of thing.'

'No,' said Freddy.

Denis drew himself up in an attempt at dignity.

'Listen to me, Freddy, and bear me witness. I won't let Nancy hang. They can't possibly hang her—why, what sort of jury would be convinced by one little bottle? No, I shall bring her home as soon as may be, and then I shall be a good husband to her, I swear it. I may be breaking my word to another, but I promise you this is the last time. From now on I shall be an honourable man.'

'I'm glad to hear it,' said Freddy. 'But what if this other of whom you speak won't go away quietly?'

'She will,' said Denis. 'She has another iron in the fire—a far more suitable one. She won't miss me for a moment.'

His head was nodding and his words were becoming increasingly slurred, and he showed signs of wanting to doze off in his chair. Freddy decided to leave him to it. He stood up and left the club, thinking hard. He had had some difficulty in distinguishing one woman from another in Denis's speech, but the conversation had given him much food for thought, and perhaps a slight sense of relief. He decided to go home and consider his next move carefully. He had intended to keep away from the police while he investigated, but now they had made an arrest it was becoming obvious to him that he would have to speak to them and tell them what he knew—or at least suspected, for he had no proof of anything, and could only make suppositions. He hoped fervently that they would be prepared to listen to him—for if they were not, then who knew what might happen next? The case had begun with two murders, but he did not wish to see it continue with a third.

CHAPTER TWENTY-THREE

THE NEXT MORNING Freddy went to call upon Larry Bendish.

'Hallo, old chap,' said Larry. 'Oughtn't you to be at work?'

'I am,' said Freddy. 'I was just on my way to somewhere else, but I thought I'd better come and see you first.'

'I say, you look rather serious,' said Larry. 'Has something happened?'

'They've arrested Nancy Beasley on suspicion of murdering Ticky Maltravers,' said Freddy.

'Good God!' said Larry in astonishment. 'Nancy? She didn't do it, did she?'

'That's what I'd like to find out,' said Freddy. 'I think probably not, but the police found a bottle of nicotine in her bag, and her name written in the poison-book of a chemist's shop on Oxford Street.'

'But that's hardly conclusive, is it? I mean to say, she might have bought it for quite innocent reasons.'

'True, but unfortunately she'd already told the police she'd never bought the stuff in her life.'

'Oh,' said Larry. 'I wonder how it got there, then.'

'So do I,' said Freddy. 'Listen, I'd like to ask you something. It's a silly question, but I'd just like to be sure.'

'Go on.'

'You didn't kill Ticky, did you?'

'I?' said Larry. 'Of course not. Whatever makes you think I did?'

'I don't know that I do. But I do know you took the flask into Babcock's that night, so you had the opportunity to put the poison into it, just as everybody else did.'

'Perhaps. But why should I want to kill him? I had no reason to.'

'Didn't you?' said Freddy, then, as Larry did not reply, went on, 'I know what Ticky was, and I know pretty much everybody had a reason to kill him.'

Larry regarded him silently.

'All right, then,' he said at length. 'I'll come clean. I wish I had killed him, and I envy the murderer for getting there first, because I can't promise I wouldn't have done it if I'd ever had the chance. But I wouldn't have poisoned him—that's a coward's way of doing things. I'd have shot him, or perhaps even strangled him with my bare hands, just to see the look on his face when he finally realized he was getting his just deserts.'

'I say, that's rather bloodthirsty,' said Freddy.

'If you know what he was then you'll know why I hated him so much,' said Larry.

'What about Weaver?'

'Who? Oh, the manservant, you mean?'

'Yes. He was proposing to take over the business after Ticky died. I suppose you didn't have anything to do with his death either?'

'Of course not.'

'Did the police ask you for an alibi?'

'No, but they asked Mother for hers, which just happens to be me. I'd been out with Ann, but she went home early, and when I got back my mother was there. That was at about ten, and they were interested in the time between then and one o'clock. So we both give each other an alibi—unless you think we both did it.'

'No, I don't think you did,' said Freddy. There was a look on his face that might have been sympathy.

'Kind of you,' said Larry. 'Was there anything else? Any other murders you'd like to pin on me while you're here?'

'No, thank you,' said Freddy. 'I think I'd better be going.'

Larry followed him out to the front door, slightly bemused at the visit.

'I'll see you later,' he said.

'Perhaps,' said Freddy. 'I'm sorry.'

'What for?'

'For the blunt questions—and other things.'

'You're being very cryptic.'

Freddy said nothing, but gave him an odd look and left. Twenty minutes later he walked into Scotland Yard and asked to speak to Inspector Entwistle. The inspector was not in, but Sergeant Bird would see him. Freddy had been hoping for this, and was slightly relieved that he would not have to hand his evidence to the stern inspector.

'Hallo,' said Sergeant Bird as Freddy entered. 'Come to tell me another tall story, have you? Don't think I don't know what you did with that flask. I can't prove it yet, but I will one of these days, just you wait.'

'Look here, sergeant,' said Freddy seriously. 'I'd like to call a truce, if you will. I've done my best not to ruin your investigation. It's just that sometimes one accidentally—er—gets in the way, so to speak. But I've something important to tell you, and I think you ought to listen to it.'

'Oh, do you, now?' said Bird.

Freddy brought out the clipping he had found in among Ticky's papers and pushed it across the desk to the sergeant, who glanced at it curiously.

'I expect you've deduced by now that Ticky Maltravers was a blackmailer,' said Freddy. 'He held secrets on all his friends, and extorted money from them in return for his silence.'

'We did have an inkling of that nature, yes,' said Bird cautiously.

'Well, naturally, in view of that fact, you could hardly expect any of them to be particularly interested in whether you caught his murderer or not. Most of them said good riddance and were happy to wash their hands of him—and Weaver, who was intending to continue with the blackmail.'

'Was he, now?' said the sergeant. 'How do you know that?'

'Because he told me so,' said Freddy.

'Was he blackmailing you?'

'Not me, no, but a number of people of my acquaintance. Now, I'm not here to tell you everybody's secrets, since they're none of my business or yours. I mean to say, it's a bit rich to have spent years paying to have one's peccadillos kept quiet, only to find the police thundering about and asking pointed questions of one when the blackmailer gets his comeuppance— especially if one had nothing to do with his death, don't you think?'

'It doesn't matter what I think,' said Bird. 'The law's the law, and killing people's against it.'

'True enough. But the idea of a desperate and unhappy victim administering justice with his own hands, and then being punished for it, doesn't sit well with me—or with you, I imagine. As a right-minded sort, I don't suppose you've shed too many tears over Ticky either.'

'Perhaps not, but it's still my duty to find out who killed him. I hope you're not about to ask us to turn a blind eye,' said the sergeant, drawing himself up.

'No, no, not at all,' Freddy hastened to assure him. 'Quite the contrary, in fact. Even though I think people ought to be entitled to be naughty in private without the police sticking their noses in, I do have the wit to understand that all these secrets may have a bearing on the murders.'

'Clever, aren't you?'

'So they tell me,' said Freddy. 'But that's beside the point. I don't want anyone to suffer unnecessarily, so in the interests of clearing up all the confusion and seeing that justice is done, I'm here to tell you I think I may know who did it—and it wasn't Mrs. Beasley.'

'And you've come to turn him in, after all you said about desperate and unhappy people?'

'Ah, now, there's the thing. Like everyone else, I expect the murderer wasn't too pleased about being blackmailed, but there's much more to it than that. I think Ticky and Weaver *were* killed to put an end to their activities, but their murders were merely incidental to the real crime. As a matter of fact, I believe the person in question is planning another murder—a cold and deliberate one this time.'

Sergeant Bird glanced curiously at the clipping Freddy had given him, then looked up.

'Go on,' he said.

CHAPTER TWENTY-FOUR

A HEAVY RAIN was falling over London when Freddy left Scotland Yard an hour or so later, thinking about his conversation with Sergeant Bird. The sergeant had listened to what he had to say, but had been discouraging, since, as he pointed out, a person's past behaviour in an entirely different case could not be taken as evidence in the present one, and there was no proof that anything untoward was planned, only a supposition. There was nothing the police could do until they had more information. Still, he gave a cautious promise that they would look into it—and especially the alibis for the night of Weaver's death, since it certainly looked as though it were a line worth investigating.

With that Freddy was forced to be content, and he left, hoping that something useful would come to light soon, for he had to admit the evidence was very slim. He returned to the office and put in several hours' work, much to the surprise of his colleagues, and then went home, with the case still on his mind. The *Clarion* had reported that Nancy Beasley had been charged with the murders of Ticky and Weaver, so it looked as though the police were sticking to their own theory—and he could hardly blame them. But he was almost sure they had got it wrong, and he racked his brains, trying to think of a way to prove it, for he had very little to go on except a strong suspicion and a missing alibi, neither of which was likely to convince a jury.

After an hour or two of pacing up and down in his room, he gave it up and decided to go out, with half a thought of visiting Charles Street again. But just as he had reached this decision, the bell rang. He answered it and found Ann Chadwick standing there, very wet.

'Hallo,' he said. 'What's this? What happened to your umbrella?'

'I came out in a hurry and forgot it,' she said.

'Then you'd better come in. The fire's rather poor, I'm afraid, as I was just about to go out.'

'Oh, I'm sorry, I didn't mean to keep you,' she said.

'As a matter of fact, you're the very person I was coming to see,' said Freddy.

'I?'

'Yes, but it doesn't matter now. Would you like me to hang your coat and hat up to dry?'

'No, thank you,' she said. She seemed to be only half-listening. She moved towards the fire and held out her hands to it, then turned suddenly and said, 'Larry says you accused him of murdering Ticky this morning.'

'That's not quite how I remember it,' said Freddy. 'As I recall, I merely inquired politely whether he had done it, since I'd just found out he had the opportunity.'

'Well, he didn't do it,' she said. 'And I think it was jolly rude of you to ask.'

'It's a touch impolite to put poison in someone's brandy, too, don't you think?'

'Of course it is, but it's none of your business. The police have it all in hand.'

'But they've arrested Nancy,' said Freddy. 'Don't tell me you think she's guilty.'

She lowered her eyes.

'I don't know what to think,' she said at last, and there was a tremble in her voice. 'I should never have believed it for a second, but the bottle was there in her bag—you saw it yourself, and then the police said she signed the poison-book. And there were other things—but I won't betray a confidence. Mrs. Beasley trusts me, and the most important thing now is to make sure she's never found guilty.'

'Oh, very good,' said Freddy. 'Yes, that's very good. Well, I can't speak for Nancy, but as things stand it certainly looks as though everything is going to be resolved to your satisfaction.'

She darted him a doubtful glance, but his expression was as bland as it could be.

'And how is Denis taking it?' he went on.

'Not well, I think,' she said. 'He's gone to stay at his club. He says he can't bear to be at home while this is all going on.'

'Still, I expect he'll soon get over it all with your assistance.'

This time there was no mistaking his tone. She frowned.

'I don't know what you mean,' she said.

'Don't you? Perhaps I've got it wrong, then. It's just that I did hear a rumour that Denis is in love with you.'

'That's nonsense,' she said sharply. 'Who told you that?'

'He did.'

'Then he had no business to. There's nothing between us. I've always kept him at arm's length, in fact. In my sort of job errant husbands are a hazard one has to put up with.'

'Yes, and you ought to know,' said Freddy.

'What are you talking about?'

'You're not too particular about other women's husbands, are you? At least, not from what I've read.'

A wary look had come into her eyes, but she said nothing.

'That's why you're really here, isn't it?' he continued. 'It's nothing to do with Larry or Nancy. You've been talking to Amelia. I ought to have warned her to keep quiet, but I didn't think to mention it. I expect she told you about our little trip to Dorking, yes?'

Still she was silent, and her eyes never left his as he went on talking.

'It seems Ticky was a busy man,' he said. 'He made quite a concern of it. Little wonder he could afford to dine as well as he did. I spent several days last week finding out a lot of people's guilty secrets—and believe me, I'd rather not have, but I wanted Ticky's victims to know they were free, and so in many cases it was unavoidable. At any rate, you may be interested to know that while I was looking through the papers we found, I saw a photograph of someone I recognized. She was a witness at the inquest into the death of a Mrs. Spencer in Bournemouth two years ago, and had been Mrs. Spencer's secretary. Some rather pointed questions were asked at the inquest, it seems. The dead woman's sister claimed that the secretary—a Miss Ann Wickham—had been carrying on an affair with Mr. Spencer, who had little money of his own, but became a rich man upon the death of his wife. Of course, people will talk, and there was some suspicion in this case that Mrs. Spencer's death had been a little too convenient. However, death was ruled to have been of natural causes, and no arrests were made. One might have assumed that after a decent interval, Mr. Spencer and Miss Wickham would have made a match of it, but it appears they didn't. I don't know why. Perhaps because mud sticks, and it's difficult to live down accusations of that sort. The case interested me, and so I made a telephone-call to the Bournemouth police, who told me—in confidence, naturally—that they were as sure as they could be that Mrs. Spencer had been helped on her way, as it were, although they couldn't prove it. They also said Miss Wickham had left Bournemouth, and they had no idea where she was now. I might have told them that she'd gone to London, but I didn't.'

'You seem to know a lot about it,' she said, and to his surprise he saw tears glistening in her eyes. One began to roll down her cheek, and she dabbed at it with the back of her hand. 'I don't expect you to understand how difficult it's been. For months and months I couldn't walk down the street without hearing remarks or seeing people whispering behind their hands about me. People I thought were my friends began to cross the street to avoid speaking to me, and the worst of it was, there was nothing I could do about it. Mrs. Spencer's sister was determined that everybody should think I was a scarlet woman and a home-wrecker and a murderer—oh, yes, I heard all those words and more, and could do nothing to defend myself, even though it was all a lie. There was nothing between Mr. Spencer and me, but he refused to speak in my favour. I was left out for the wolves, so what could I do but run away? I got the job with Mrs. Beasley, and then Larry and I got engaged, and I thought I should be happy at last.'

'But then Ticky found out about you,' said Freddy.

'Yes. I don't know how, but he did. He said if I didn't give him money he'd tell Larry and the Beasleys all about me, so I had no choice but to pay up. You can't imagine how frightened I was all those months. And then Ticky was murdered, and after that his manservant, and I was so relieved—I won't deny it—and hoped so very much that I was free now. He had a newspaper clipping with my picture on it, and I was rather worried about it, but I hoped the police would be tactful enough not to tell everyone about it if they found it. And then Amelia said you and she had found a bundle of papers, and I thought about it and thought about it for days, wondering whether to come and ask you for the clipping, and in the end I decided you were a kind sort, so here I am.'

'Poor you,' said Freddy. 'It sounds as though you've had a rough time of it.'

She looked up hopefully.

'Or, at least, that's what I should say if I believed a word of it,' he went on. 'But nothing doing, I'm afraid. You tell a pretty story, but I know an accomplished liar when I see one.'

She drew in her breath.

'I thought you had a good heart,' she said. 'It seems I was wrong.'

'I'm kindly enough disposed towards those who deserve it,' he said. 'But you seem to forget Nancy.'

'Nancy?'

'Yes. You remember? Nancy, your employer, who is currently languishing in gaol, waiting to find out whether they're going to hang her. Rather unfortunate for her, don't you think?'

'I can't help that. She was one of Ticky's victims too, and decided to take justice into her own hands, just as any of us might have done. I'm sure plenty of people were desperate enough to try it.'

'I'm sure they were, but that doesn't mean they did it,' said Freddy. 'But I think Ticky's murder was only a small part of a larger plan. Nancy's a wealthy woman. Her father was a millionaire, and if she does hang, then Denis is going to be very rich. And he's in love with you, which makes this a perfect opportunity. If at first you don't succeed, try, try again, what? You didn't quite pull it off with Mr. Spencer, but there's no need to waste a perfectly good idea just because it didn't work the first time.'

'You're quite mad,' said Ann.

'Am I? Let me tell you what I know or can guess: you came to Nancy shortly after her father died and left her lots of money.

The Beasleys appeared in the gossip pages often enough, so you already knew about Denis's little weakness, and set out to work on him and make him fall in love with you. Now, it would be no use at all if Nancy divorced Denis, since she was the one with the money and would have left him penniless if the marriage had ended in court. What you really needed was for her to die conveniently, so that Denis would inherit everything. I can't prove it, of course, but I think you planned to kill Nancy sooner or later, leaving the way clear for you to land yourself a rich husband. I don't know where Larry came in, but I think perhaps you were frightened that people would suspect funny business between you and Denis, and start talking, as they did in Bournemouth. After all, it's talk that prevented you from marrying this Spencer chap, and you wanted to avoid the same thing happening again, so you accepted a handy proposal from a respectable young man to draw attention away from your real purpose while you worked on your plan.

'Unfortunately for you, Ticky rather got in the way when he found out about your past and started blackmailing you. But you're a clever girl, and came up with a way to kill two birds with one stone, so to speak: you decided to kill Ticky and pin the blame on Nancy—a much more ingenious scheme than simply murdering her would have been, since sudden deaths tend to arouse the interest of the police, and you'd already had trouble with that sort of thing. So you prepared the ground by buying a bottle of nicotine and signing your name as Nancy Beasley. After that you bought the flask, put a few drops of nicotine in it and wrapped it up. Then Nancy forgot it and nearly ruined the whole thing, and you had to send it into the restaurant after her. Of course, you had no way of knowing whether your plan would work, but you rightly thought that if Ticky did drink from the flask, then the police would concentrate on the people who were there at Babcock's that night. After Ticky died, I expect you tried to get the clipping back. Weaver told me he'd had a few visitors, but that he'd sent them away and told them business would continue as normal. All you could do then was to wait for the opportunity to get into the house and kill him. I suppose he let you in when you told him you'd come to pay him?'

Ann said nothing, and Freddy continued:

'After that, you searched the house, but found nothing, because Weaver had hidden the documents at his mother's place. Then you waited for the police to find enough evidence to arrest Nancy. It was a good plan, by the way. I didn't suspect you at all until I found that cutting, and even then I didn't immediately assume that you'd done it, since all the article showed was that Ticky had been blackmailing you, and that you had a motive for killing him in the same way as everybody else. I dare say you won't believe me, but I've been struggling with my conscience for the past week, wondering whether to let the matter lie, since I didn't want the responsibility of reporting someone to the police who had done the world a good turn by ridding it of someone very unpleasant. I don't know what I'd have decided in the end, but you made up my mind for me when you tried to throw the blame on to Nancy. I was watching you when the police arrested her, and

I saw your face. I've never seen such a look of triumph. It was almost indecent. You bought that poison and planted the bottle in her bag so the police would find it, didn't you?'

'I've never heard such a lot of nonsense,' said Ann at last. 'Of course it's not true—and even if it were, you've no proof.'

'No,' said Freddy. 'Although I do happen to know you have no alibi for the time of Weaver's murder. Larry said you and he were out together that night, but he left you before ten and went home. Denis, meanwhile, says he got home at eleven and nobody was there, although one would have expected you to have come straight home after you left Larry. Where were you?'

'I don't remember,' she said. She was beginning to sound a little rattled. 'Don't ask me that. I won't give him away.'

'Won't give who away?' he said. 'Are you trying to make me believe this was all Denis's idea? My word, you'll seize any opportunity you can to get yourself out of trouble, won't you? As a matter of fact, I did think at first that you might both be in on it, but then I spoke to Denis at his club last night, and heard a lot of things I expect he wouldn't have dreamed of telling me had he been sober. *In vino veritas*, and all that. He's pretty horrified at Nancy's arrest, and suffering from what I can only describe as a fever of guilt. I hate to be the bearer of bad news, but he told me that he's going to stand by Nancy, and has decided to end things with you. He wasn't too worried about you, as he seems to think you're sincere in your feelings for Larry and will be happy enough with him.'

At that she gave an angry little gasp, but quickly mastered herself and lifted her chin.

'I can see you're trying to provoke me into some sort of confession,' she said. 'But it won't work, because you've got it all wrong. I didn't murder Ticky or Weaver, and I'm certainly not trying to blame Nancy for it. You're just making wild accusations with no proof. If you're so sure I did it, then why don't you go to the police? Or have you already spoken to them?'

Freddy hesitated, then came to a reckless decision.

'No,' he said at last. 'They don't know anything about this. I didn't want to mention it to them until I'd spoken to you and found out the truth.'

At that her expression softened, and she came a little closer to him.

'I *am* telling the truth,' she said, and there was a ring of sincerity in her voice. 'I promise you I had nothing to do with all this. I wished Ticky out of the way as much as anyone, but I should never have done anything about it. I grumbled and paid up, just like everybody else. And I'm perfectly devastated about Nancy's arrest. Perhaps it doesn't seem that way, but I'm not the emotional sort—I never was. I don't lose my temper or burst into tears when things go wrong. I'm the sort who thinks things through carefully and doesn't do anything hasty. Look here, I don't know whether Nancy killed him or not, but I promise you I intend to do everything in my power to make sure she isn't convicted. She's been so terribly good to me that I should be nothing but ungrateful if I didn't try to help her as much as I can. Please, Freddy, say you believe me. I should hate you to think badly of me.'

She was gazing at him appealingly. Freddy looked at her standing there, so calm, intelligent and competent, dressed neatly and smartly as always, and wondered how anyone could believe her to be a murderess. If she were ever to stand in the dock, surely no jury would ever convict her on the present evidence. Why, it was inconceivable. He sighed and gave her a rueful smile.

'Well, if you are innocent, all I can say is that you've made some pretty spiteful enemies,' he said at last. 'Even the papers in Bournemouth seem to have taken every opportunity to print nasty rumours about you.'

She winced.

'Yes, they were rather horrid,' she said. 'It was very upsetting.' She paused. 'Does this mean you believe me, then?'

'I don't see how anyone could doubt you,' he said. 'You'll forgive me for saying all those things, won't you? But I had to be sure.'

'Thank you,' she said in a low voice. 'I'm so glad.'

There was a silence, then Freddy said:

'I think the rain has stopped. Let me lend you an umbrella for the way home.'

'There's no need. I shall be quite all right,' she said, and moved towards the door, then hesitated, as though struck by a thought. 'I don't suppose you still have that cutting, do you?' she said tentatively. 'I'd be awfully grateful if you'd give it to me—or at least destroy it.'

It was now that Freddy braced himself to do something either very brave or very foolish.

'Oh, yes, I think I have it here somewhere,' he said. 'Now, where did I put it?'

And so saying, he turned his back, his heart thumping, and made as if to root among a little pile of papers that lay on a bookshelf just behind him. Also on the shelf was a silver trophy for some sporting achievement or other—one of the very few he had won at school. It was kept well polished, and he looked into it and watched, holding his breath, as the distorted reflection of Ann Chadwick put its hand into its pocket and crept silently towards him. When he whirled around, there was the knife, raised and ready to strike. Quick as a flash he dodged to one side just as it came down, but he was not quite fast enough, and the blade caught him on his left upper arm. At first he was aware of no pain, only a warm, sticky wetness as the blood began to seep through his sleeve, and he grimaced as Ann gave a little scream of frustration.

'Oh, no you don't,' he said, and made a grab for the knife. She jumped back and swiped at him again, but she had lost the element of surprise now, and ran to put a chair between them.

'Give that to me,' said Freddy. 'You don't think I'm just going to let you stick it in me, do you?'

He circled around the chair after her. A frightened look came into her eyes, and she seemed to be on the point of retreating. He felt he had the upper hand, and was preparing to make a rush at her and take the knife from her, when she made a sudden lunge forward with it pointed at his heart. He leapt back just in time, and it missed him by an inch.

'Why, you—' he said, outraged that she had fooled him so easily.

Now she was becoming desperate, for she knew there was no way out for her if she left him alive. She gave a sort of growl, and began to stab the knife repeatedly in his direction, pressing forward even as he retreated. Her eyes were wide, and her expression was one of concentrated fury, and she seemed as unlike the usual calm, serene Ann Chadwick as it was possible to be. Freddy began to think he ought to make a run for it, for she did not look as though she would give up her weapon lightly, and his arm was beginning to throb with pain. However, she had cut a great gash in his favourite jacket, which irked him more than it ought to have in the circumstances, and made him perversely determined to get the knife off her by hook or by crook. He was bigger than she, of course, and had the advantage of greater physical strength, so it ought to have been fairly easy for him, even with his injured arm, to overpower her. However, he was hampered by a lifetime's drilling in good manners, which had taught him that it was not permitted to hit a woman, and so he wasted a good few minutes in trying to grab hold of her wrist—a dangerous enterprise, which very nearly led to his losing a finger or two. At last she forced his hand by making a lunge at him that nearly slit his throat, upon which he abandoned his manners, threw himself at her, and brought her down with all his weight. She screamed as they hit the floor, but still would not let go of the knife, and he was surprised at her strength as he tried to prise it from her hand. For a few moments they grappled, and he was so caught up in the struggle that he did not hear the sound of a key in the lock, and was unaware that anybody had come in until he heard a shriek.

'Freddy! What on *earth* do you think you're doing?' came Cynthia's horrified voice. 'Let go of her at once!'

At her words, Freddy glanced around, saw his mother standing in the doorway, a folded umbrella in her hand, and loosened his grip—just long enough to allow Ann to take advantage of his momentary lapse in attention and take a swipe at his shoulder. The blade went in a little way and he gave a yell. At that, Ann wriggled out from underneath him and scrabbled away from him on her hands and knees.

'Stop her!' exclaimed Freddy as he saw her heading for the door.

Cynthia was starting to realize that she had gravely misread the situation. She stared at Freddy, who was clutching his bleeding shoulder and trying to sit up, and then at Ann.

'You've stabbed him!' she said in outraged disbelief. 'How dare you? Oh, no you don't,' she said, spurred suddenly into action, her one thought to prevent the woman who had injured her only darling son from making good her escape. Before Ann could get up, Cynthia stepped forward and struck her smartly over the head with the umbrella once, then twice. Ann cried out and dropped the knife as she put her hands over her head to shield herself, and Cynthia picked it up.

'You oughtn't to carry this sort of thing around,' she said. 'You might hurt someone.'

Freddy struggled to his feet and went to lock the front door, watching Ann warily all the while.

'You'd better give the knife to me,' he said grimly. 'I don't trust her an inch.'

'Shall I call the police?' said Cynthia, eyeing the telephone.

'Do,' said Freddy. 'She killed Ticky and she's been trying to pin the blame on Nancy.'

'Goodness me!' said Cynthia. 'That won't do at all.'

She picked up the receiver and asked for the police. Freddy went across and looked down at Ann, who was still kneeling on the floor, glaring furiously at first one of them, then the other.

'If you'll sit quietly until the police come I won't tie your wrists,' he said. 'But it's not very comfortable down there. Why don't you sit in a chair?'

Ann said nothing, but turned her face away from him. Her murderous energy seemed spent, but he knew what she was capable of, and had no intention of taking his eyes off her. The pain in his arm and shoulder was getting worse, and he wanted to get his wounds seen to, but he could not until the prisoner had been taken away, and so he sat down, and the three of them waited in silence for the police to arrive.

CHAPTER TWENTY-FIVE

THE NEXT FEW days were busy ones for Freddy. First, his arm needed attention; although he was in some pain, he was relieved to hear that the wounds were fairly superficial, and would heal nicely with care and a little rest. After that, he spent some time in conference with the men of Scotland Yard, who were now inclined to take his view of the case, since well-bred young ladies did not, as a rule, tend to visit young men in their own homes with a view to stabbing them in the back, and so it could be fairly inferred that this was a matter that required investigation. Ann Chadwick had been arrested on a charge of attempted murder, and evidence was now beginning to come to light that seemed to show she was also responsible for the deaths of Ticky Maltravers and James Weaver. The proprietor of the chemist's shop from which the nicotine had been purchased could not positively identify the person who had bought the poison, but the signature in the poison-book—although a fair imitation—was certainly not that of Nancy Beasley. Then the knife Ann had brought with her to kill Freddy was shown to be one of a pair—the other having been used to murder Weaver. Furthermore, she could not or would not say where she had been on the night of Weaver's death—and in fact, was maintaining a stubborn silence in the face of any attempts to question her. All in all, there seemed no further reason to continue holding Mrs. Beasley in prison, and so she was released, to her very great joy.

'I don't recommend these sorts of goings-on, sir,' said Sergeant Bird on Wednesday afternoon. He had come to Freddy's flat to examine the scene of the fight, and had found Freddy lounging artistically on a sofa with his bandage arranged to its greatest advantage. 'You might have been killed.'

'True,' said Freddy. 'But think of the time and effort I've saved you. Why, if I hadn't lured her into my trap, the thing might have dragged on for months, since I refuse to believe a judge would have done anything but throw out the case against Mrs. Beasley on such flimsy evidence.'

'There's not a *great* deal of evidence against Miss Chadwick, either,' said Bird. 'If she hadn't tried to kill you, then we might have had difficulty in prosecuting anybody at all. I suppose we ought to thank you, even if it was a very foolish thing to do on your part.'

'Yes, it occurred to me as soon as she hacked a hole in my arm that perhaps I'd bitten off a little more than I could chew. It's not the sort of thing I'd normally do. In fact, to be perfectly frank, I can't think what got into me.'

'A knife, sir.'

'Oh, very good,' said Freddy appreciatively. 'Do they teach you jokes like that at police school? Would they accept me, do you think?'

'I beg your pardon, but a policeman is required to demonstrate evidence of good character and high moral standing—at least, I seem to remember that's what they call it.'

'Are you suggesting I lack those qualities, sergeant?'

'I couldn't say, sir. Which reminds me: you don't happen to know anything about the child's toy cart we found while we were searching Mrs. Pilkington-Soames's house, do you?'

Freddy raised his eyebrows politely.

'A child's toy cart, you say? Why, no, I don't think so. I used to have something of the kind myself, but I thought it had been thrown away long ago. Is it still there?'

'It is indeed,' said the sergeant.

'Were you thinking of taking it down Parliament Hill?' said Freddy. 'I doubt it would hold your weight.'

'Probably not. But it's had *something* heavy in it lately, by the looks of it. There are several cracks in the wood that look very recent.'

'Perhaps someone's been carrying coal in it,' suggested Freddy.

'Not coal, I don't think,' said Bird. 'But I'm pretty certain someone's been pushing it about in the street. There were some flecks of dried black paint on it that looked as though they might have come from the railings in Eaton Terrace—or possibly even Caroline Terrace.'

'How very odd.'

'It is, isn't it?'

'Still, I don't suppose it has anything to do with the murder,' said Freddy. 'After all, we know who did it.'

'But there are still some things we don't know. For instance, two doctors have sworn that Mr. Maltravers' body was moved after he died.'

'Yes, I remember you said something of the sort. Might they have made a mistake?'

'Not likely, is it?' said Bird.

'Well, then, perhaps someone found him in the street and decided to move him out of the way for one reason or another. It was probably something quite innocent, and nothing to worry about.'

'Perhaps not, but it confused the investigation no end. If we'd found him where he died then we might have solved the case much more quickly.'

'Still, no harm done, eh?' said Freddy. 'You found the murderer and we can all go on as we were before.'

'That's as may be, but I might hope that whoever was responsible for moving the body would have the sense in future not to interfere with the police in the carrying-out of their duty,' said Bird with some emphasis.

'Oh, I agree with you absolutely,' said Freddy sincerely. 'But as I think I said to you before, sometimes people accidentally get in the way, and it can't be helped.'

Having demonstrated to his satisfaction that he was not to be taken for a fool, Sergeant Bird shortly afterwards went away, leaving Freddy to trust that the subject of Ticky Maltravers' final journey might never be brought up again. He was feeling tired, and was just settling himself back against the cushions in preparation for a nap, when his mother arrived.

'What are you doing, lolling about at this time of day?' she said. 'Oughtn't you to be up by now?'

'I was feeling a little weak,' he replied. 'Loss of blood, you know. It makes one rather tired.'

'Nonsense. It was barely a scratch, and you've had ages to recover. Listen, I've come because I need your help. Marjorie Belcher is holding an afternoon tea today for her saved women in Clerkenwell, and Nancy and I were supposed to be setting everything up in the church hall, but of course Nancy can't do it now, so you'll have to come with me instead.'

'Why can't Nancy do it? I thought she'd been released.'

'So she has, but Denis is whisking her off to the Riviera for the winter, so she won't be doing any of this sort of thing for a while,' said Cynthia. 'I'm rather cross with her for leaving it all to me, as a matter of fact. I only got in with Mrs. Belcher in the first place because Nancy begged me, and now she's left me in the lurch, and I'm afraid there won't be enough helpers to keep an eye on things. If you ask me, it's a waste of time trying to help these women, anyway. Most of them only come for the free tea and cakes, and I'm perfectly convinced they go back to drinking as soon as they get home. And I'm not entirely sure they're all as honest as they'd like us to believe. There's one girl in particular I shall be keeping my eye on, who has an especially wicked look about her. I had to speak to her for insubordination at the reception the other week, and she was most impertinent. Then afterwards we found quite a few spoons and things were missing. I can't prove it was her, but she's the brazen sort so I shouldn't be a bit surprised.'

'If she was stealing the silver then I don't suppose she'll be back,' said Freddy, who had a suspicion as to the identity of the young woman to whom his mother was referring. He wondered, not for the first time, why Valentina Sangiacomo was pretending to be down on her luck and accepting Mrs. Belcher's charity, for he was sure she had no need of anything of the sort—and, indeed, seemed perfectly capable of looking after herself without anyone's patronage. He resolved that if he ever met her again he would find out all he could about her, for she struck him as a most interesting individual, and a person worth knowing—provided he kept a hand on his pocket-book whenever she were near.

'Anyway, I must go, darling,' said Cynthia. 'I'm glad to see you're on the mend—although of course it serves you right, since you really oughtn't to be inviting girls here even if they're not planning to kill you.'

'I didn't—' began Freddy, but she was not listening, and went on:

'I know we're all very modern these days, but it's not quite the done thing, and you might get into trouble if you're not careful. In my day there'd have been the most awful to-do if my father had found me visiting young men without a chaperone. Not that I'd have dreamed of it, of course, but there was *one* young man who was rather insistent. Very handsome, too, as I remember. However, it's a good thing your father stepped in first, as the other one lost both his legs in the war, and if I'd married him then we wouldn't be sitting here now, would we?

Now, you'd better not lie there all morning. I shall come back at two and we'll go to this place together. You'll be no good for hanging bunting with that arm of yours, but I dare say you can hold a teapot.'

And with that she departed as briskly as she arrived, leaving Freddy to fall into a comfortable doze.

CHAPTER TWENTY-SIX

ON FRIDAY, FREDDY went to Curzon Street to see Lady Bendish. She received him with some surprise—which quickly turned to fear when he dropped a hint as to the purpose of his visit.

'Is this never to end?' she said, as he brought out the clipping which showed beyond all doubt that her first husband had been alive and well still even after her second husband, Sir Henry Bendish, had died.

'I hope it will end here,' said Freddy, and handed her the article. 'It's none of my business, and you have nothing to fear from me. I'm only sorry it went on for so long.'

She stared at him in mistrust.

'But are you—' she said. 'I mean, you've read it, I suppose?'

'I'm afraid I have,' said Freddy. 'I'm sorry. Ticky died, and it was a motive for murder, you see, so I had to. But I promise you I've told no-one else, and nor will I. I shall forget it as soon as I can, in fact.'

'I wish I could,' she said. 'But this whole thing has caused so much pain to everyone that I don't know whether I shall ever get over it.'

'I'm so awfully sorry about Ann,' said Freddy. 'Sorry for Larry, I mean. I expect he's dreadfully cut up about it, is he?'

'He is, rather,' she said. 'My poor boy. It's been a shock to us all.'

'I wish it hadn't all turned out the way it did,' said Freddy. 'I mean to say, I might have let things well alone, but I couldn't let an innocent person take the blame.'

'No, of course not. That wouldn't have been right,' she said. 'And I understand she was quite violent in the end.'

'Yes,' he said, wincing slightly.

'How is your arm, by the way?'

'A little sore, but I'll mend.'

There was a silence, as she looked down at the cutting which had been the cause of so much anguish for so long.

'Tear it up,' suggested Freddy.

She glanced up at him, then almost hesitantly did as he said. She tore it into halves, then quarters, then eighths, and then kept on tearing until she had a handful of tiny scraps of paper, like confetti.

'There,' he said. 'As though it never existed.'

'Thank you,' she said sincerely.

'You're very welcome. And now, if you don't mind, I think I'd better make myself scarce before Larry gets back. I don't suppose he's exactly pleased with me at the moment.'

'He's upset, but it couldn't be helped.'

'Still, there's no need to rub it in by intruding my presence upon you more than necessary,' he said.

She tried to thank him again but he waved it away and departed, leaving her to stare mournfully out of the window. It was too much to say that she felt relief, for there was always the risk that someone else would find out her secret one day, but for now she trusted she was safe. The past could not be put right, now that both of her husbands were dead, but were she ever to marry again—and she was a handsome woman still, so it was not beyond hope—she should tell the truth to her new husband, that she might never again be exposed to such unpleasantness.

Here, her thoughts turned involuntarily to a dinner she had attended the previous evening, during which she had received a number of politely admiring glances from a Swiss gentleman who was engaged in the business of importing and exporting precious metals, and she smiled gently.

FREDDY'S NEXT STOP was Dover Street. He knocked at a certain number, and the door was opened by a brown-skinned manservant, who at length informed him that Captain Atherton would be pleased to see him. He led Freddy up a flight of stairs and into a large living-room which was unmistakably masculine, for the walls were hung with swords and axes, and other odd wooden artifacts, and the heads of exotic animals, and photographs of natives and elephants and straw huts, while every surface seemed covered with globes and maps and logbooks and journals. In one corner was a large, leather trunk, while in another was an enormous curved tube, seemingly fashioned from the trunk of a small tree, and decorated with brightly-coloured woven cords. Whether it were a ceremonial weapon or a musical instrument, Freddy could not tell.

Captain Atherton rose from his chair as Freddy came in, and held out a hand.

'Mrs. Pilkington-Soames's boy, aren't you?' he said.

'Yes, sir,' said Freddy.

'Sit down, if you like,' said Atherton. There was a wary look on his face, and Freddy wondered if he suspected something. He had noticed that on a table by Atherton's chair lay a shiny revolver. It did nothing to ease his nervousness.

'Thank you,' he said, and did so. There was no sense in beating about the bush, so he took a deep breath, and said: 'I've come to return your letters.'

'My letters?' said Atherton. He seemed to stiffen. 'Which letters?'

'The ones Ticky was using to blackmail you,' said Freddy. 'He wasn't doing it only to you, by the way. I happen to know he had lots of people in his clutches. And I also know that his manservant, Weaver, was intending to continue with the business. He told me so himself.'

'Ah. He got you, too, did he?' said Atherton. 'I had no idea he'd made such a general concern of it.'

'Not me. But friends of mine,' said Freddy. 'I don't like that sort of thing, so I thought I'd scout about a bit and see if I could discover what Ticky and Weaver were hiding, before the police found it all and started making a nuisance of themselves.'

'I tried that myself—or rather, Mahomet did,' said Atherton. 'But there was nothing doing. It wasn't kept in the house.'

'Oh, was that you?' said Freddy. 'I'm sorry to say your man was spotted by a tramp.'

'Indeed? That was careless of him. Ought I to tell him to disappear for a while?'

'I don't think there's any need,' said Freddy. 'The man in question can barely remember his own name most of the time. The police would never be stupid enough to put him in the witness-box.'

'Good,' said Atherton. 'I shouldn't like to have to do without him.'

'At any rate,' went on Freddy, 'I wanted to find whatever Ticky was keeping before the police did, since it didn't seem fair that everyone's secrets should come out when only one person murdered him, so I employed somebody to keep an eye on Weaver. Fortunately, he led us to the hiding-place before he died. A good thing, too, or someone else might have got hold of it all.'

Atherton was sitting up rather straighter now, and his expression was wooden. Freddy, feeling most uncomfortable, continued:

'I've spent the past few days sending back letters and documents to all the people who lost them. It's been a queasy business, all told, but I thought it ought to be done. I sent them back with a note to say that all accounts had been settled.'

'Kind of you,' said Atherton.

Freddy reached into his pocket and brought out a small sheaf of letters, all written in the same crabbed scrawl, and handed them to the other man.

'These are yours, I believe,' he said.

Atherton glanced down at the papers.

'Yes,' he said. 'Have you told anyone about them?'

Freddy glanced at the revolver. Feeling once again that he was taking his life in his hands, even though Ticky's murderer had been caught, he decided to tell the truth.

'No,' he said. 'Nobody knows about them except me.'

'And you haven't come to continue the business?'

'Certainly not. The letters aren't mine. I haven't the slightest interest in them. They're yours, and you can count on my silence. I give you my word.'

He made as if to rise, but Captain Atherton held up a hand.

'One moment,' he said. 'Since you evidently know all, I should like to tell you that I'm not such a coward and a fraud as you may think—or rather, I've been both of those things, but no longer. I've lived with the lie for some years now, but it's time to tell the truth. You've read the letters?'

'Yes,' admitted Freddy.

'Then you'll know it wasn't I who discovered the Injinka tribe, but a young Austrian student by the name of Heinrich Schmidt.'

'That's what he said,' said Freddy cautiously.

'Oh, it was all true enough,' said Captain Atherton. 'He found the tribe first, and led me to them, then disappeared for months. I thought he was dead, so I came home and claimed all the credit for the discovery, although I'd had nothing to do with it. I was hailed a hero, a second Dr. Livingstone, and bedecked with honours and awards. But it was all a sham, of course. Schmidt turned up eventually, ready to tell the world of what he had discovered, only to find that I'd already laid claim to it. What was he to do? I was the famous explorer—discoverer of the remains of the lost Cushite city of Kedzala; the only white man to undergo the ancient initiation rituals of the jungle peoples of the Maroban Islands; the first to reach corners of the earth we never before knew existed—whereas he was nobody. At first he didn't quite believe I'd done it. He sent a letter full of polite doubts and requests for me to give him the credit that was due to him, but by then I was too caught up with the fame and adulation to be willing to give it up easily. I lived in fear of exposure, but I knew the sort of man he was—knew he was tremendously modest and not the kind to make a fuss, and so I took the risk, and bet that he would keep quiet about it. I ignored his letters, and at length he stopped writing. Afterwards, I found out he'd died, and breathed a sigh of relief. It was shortly after that that Maltravers got hold of the letters from that manservant of his, who stole them from me during a house party, and began demanding money in return for my silence. Of course I paid up—what else could I do? It was either that or face exposure. Then the two of them were murdered and I ought to have been happy, but I wasn't. I lost the ability to be happy a long time ago, when I gave up honour and decency in favour of glory. But now I've decided it's time to tell the truth.'

'Oh?' said Freddy.

'Yes. It's all in my memoirs. I finished them a few weeks ago and had been about to send them off, but I changed my mind at the last minute and added a chapter, in which I give Heinrich Schmidt full credit for the discovery that made me the most celebrated explorer of the age. I sent the book to my publisher this morning. I expect it will cause something of a stir. Of course, you'll say I ought to have done it long ago—and you're quite right, but better late than never, I suppose.'

'That's rather a brave thing to do, sir,' said Freddy.

'Don't call me brave. I'm sure I don't need to tell you about the self-disgust I've felt ever since I took that first fatal step along the road to perdition. In the end, confessing will be no harder than living with the lie has been.'

He fell silent, and Freddy found himself lost for words. He had done what he set out to do, and returned Captain Atherton's documents to him so that he might keep his secret if he wished, but it seemed Atherton could no longer stomach the idea of what he had become, and was proposing to create an enormous scandal by admitting the truth at last. Freddy had no idea whether Atherton was doing the right thing, but it was not for him to try and persuade him into one course of action or the other, so after a minute or two he got up and took his leave.

The captain was staring straight ahead, and barely seemed to notice as Freddy bade him goodbye and went out, but after a few minutes he came to himself. He stood up and looked out of the window until Freddy was out of sight, then returned to his armchair, sat down, and picked up the revolver that was sitting on the table next to him. Freddy need not have worried that he was in danger, for Atherton had quite another purpose in mind for the gun. He had lived a life of great daring and intrepidity—a good, active life, all told. He had added to the sum of human knowledge, and would be remembered for many discoveries, although of course they would now all be overshadowed by his disgrace. He had achieved all that he was ever likely to achieve, and so what was the use in sitting and waiting for the blow to fall, for the humiliation to be heaped upon him? No; it was much better this way. He should put an end to it all now and let the world think of him as it would.

He raised the revolver and put it to his temple, then, before he could change his mind, pulled the trigger. There was a click, and he lowered the gun and stared at it in puzzlement, for he knew he had loaded it only that morning. But now it was empty. He was still regarding it when he felt a presence at his shoulder and looked up to see Mahomet, his faithful servant, standing there.

'Did you do this?' he said.

Mahomet bowed his head.

'Yes, sir,' he said.

'Why?'

'Because you are not ready to die,' said Mahomet.

'And what if I say I am? What if I say I don't wish to remain here while the world vilifies me and abuses my very name—and justifiably so?'

'It was an error on your part,' said Mahomet. 'Are we not all entitled to make a mistake?'

Atherton gave a short laugh.

'It was more than that,' he said. 'It was deliberate dishonesty. I deserve to be publicly disgraced.'

'You will be punished,' acknowledged Mahomet. 'It is inevitable. You did wrong, and everyone will know it. But think of all the right you have done, too—all the things you have discovered, all your past kindnesses. I have not forgotten how you rescued me from those robbers, who would surely have killed me had you not arrived in time to see them off. And not only that; I have seen many, many other instances of your generosity and goodwill. Do you not remember how you single-handedly evacuated an entire Indian village and saved all its inhabitants from dangerous flood waters when the dam burst in a storm? Think of all the innocent women and children who would have died had you not remained until the very end, to clear out every last house, at great risk to your own life. Those people are ignorant and illiterate; they do not write letters to newspapers, but even today they will praise your very name to the skies. And there are many more such stories. Do not waste such a life by ending it here in London, where people have nothing better to do than judge you for one moment of madness.'

'Then what do you suggest I do?'

'There is a boat that sails for Cape Town in two days. Let us take it and return to the life that suits you best, far away from all this.'

Atherton stared at his manservant for a few moments, then turned his head to look out of the window. Outside all was grey and wet. He thought of the heat, and the sun, and the dust, and the smells, and the noise, and the gay colours of Africa, and felt a pang of the old longing. Mahomet was right: he had been too long in London, and he did not really wish to die while there was life, and excitement, and adventure still to be had. Perhaps a bullet to the head was not the only way out, after all.

'Do you think we might be ready in time?' he said.

'I have already begun packing, sir,' said Mahomet.

FREDDY'S LAST STOP was Brook Street, where Blanche Van Leeuwen lived. He found her curled up on the sofa in her cat-like way, reading a magazine. In the grey afternoon half-light she looked not a day older than thirty.

'Hallo, Freddy,' she said in her usual languid drawl, as he entered her well-appointed sitting-room. 'Are you looking for Amelia? She's gone to see Lady Bendish, or so she says.'

'Oh?' said Freddy.

'Yes. Of course, it's all nonsense. She's really gone to hang around Larry. They were quite the sweet little girl-and-boy-friend at one time, you know. For a while I thought he was going to take her off my hands for good, but then the Chadwick girl came along and stole him from under her nose and she had to pretend not to care. She'll get him this time, though.'

'Do you think so?' said Freddy, disconcerted. 'I thought he was inconsolable.'

'Don't be silly. No man is inconsolable. She'll listen to him and comfort him and praise him and agree with everything he says, and he'll simply lap it up. Just you watch. If they're not engaged by the spring then I'm a Dutchman.'

This was a disappointment, but Freddy bore the blow as philosophically as he could. Amelia was a sweet girl, and undoubtedly very pretty, but she was not the only pretty girl in London, for everywhere he looked he seemed to see lovely faces and bewitching smiles—sometimes even directed at him. Moreover, he felt obliquely as though he owed Larry Bendish something in return for having deprived him of his fiancée—and what better than a new fiancée? One, moreover, who was not burdened with an inconveniently murderous past. And so Freddy resigned himself to the inevitable.

'As a matter of fact, I came to see you,' he said. He brought out the last cutting, which he had kept carefully hidden from Amelia, and handed it to Blanche.

'What's this?' she said, and glanced at it. 'Ah! You found it. And you've come to give it back to me.'

'Yes,' said Freddy. 'I don't know why you wanted it kept hidden. It's nothing to be ashamed of.'

'I'm not ashamed of it,' she said. 'But when one's face is one's fortune, it's only sensible to keep an eye on one's public image, don't you think? When I came to England everybody knew me as Blanche de Montmorency of Sydney, one of the last descendants of the ancient French family of aristocrats. Of course I had the looks, but it was the name that got me into the highest social circles. How far do you think I'd have got if they'd known I was plain old Lizzie Atwell, the second daughter of a sheep farmer from Harper Springs? Beauty will get one so far, but here in London it's family that counts, so I decided to invent a better one.'

She was looking at him with an expression that held any amount of mischief. It was perfectly evident that she felt no guilt at all at her deception.

'But you paid Ticky to keep it quiet.'

'Oh, yes,' she said. 'I bargained hard, though. I told him exactly how much it was worth to me to buy his silence, and it wasn't anywhere near what he wanted, but he had to agree in the end. To tell you the truth, I didn't much care whether he told anybody or not—or rather, shall we say I was mostly worried he'd tell your ghastly mother, and she'd put it in the paper. I'm sorry, darling, I'm sure she's delightful underneath it all.'

'Well, you've nothing to worry about now,' said Freddy. 'I promise I won't tell a soul.'

'You're a good boy, Freddy,' she said. She sat up and placed the cutting in an ash-tray, then carefully set light to it. They watched as it curled and blackened in the flames. 'There. It's gone. I know I said I didn't care, but Amelia would have been very disappointed in me, and I shouldn't have liked that. I'm terribly fond of her, really.'

'I'm glad to hear it,' he said.

She looked at his left arm, which he was holding a little stiffly, for it was still very uncomfortable.

'And so I understand you caught the murderer single-handedly, and were stabbed for your pains,' she said. 'Tell me, were you very brave?'

'Not *terribly* brave,' he said modestly.

'Well, I'm glad you weren't too badly hurt. And I'm sorry if you're heartbroken over Amelia—but really, darling, you'd have found her company dreadfully wearing after a while. She has no sophistication at all, and she *squeals* so. It gives one quite a headache.'

'I don't mind,' he said. 'I expect she'd have found me a little difficult, too. I try to be good, but I'm afraid I don't always behave as well as I ought.'

'That's true enough,' she said, amused. An idea seemed to strike her, and she glanced at him speculatively. 'Look here, why don't you stay to tea? Amelia won't be back for hours yet, and I shall be awfully bored without company.'

Freddy hesitated. There was nothing in the question itself, or in the tone of her voice, but he knew exactly what she was about. He had only intended to drop in quickly, for despite his injured arm he was still meant to be working. This afternoon he was supposed to go and speak to a member of the County Council about a new drainage scheme for the Thames. He knew the man in question would bring out plans and drawings and talk at length about channels and sluices, and he would be expected to pay attention. It promised to be frightfully dull, but Mr. Bickerstaffe would give him another carpeting if he missed the appointment. It was time he started to take his duties as a reporter more seriously if he wished to get on. He opened his mouth to say as much, then saw Blanche regarding him invitingly with those wide blue eyes, so like her daughter's, but without any of the innocence. She was much nicer to look at—and much easier company—than the elderly Mr. Repton, with his dry, croaking voice and his rheumy eyes, and his enthusiasm for the finer points of sewerage.

There was a pause.

'Perhaps I might stay just a *little* while,' he said at last.

New Releases

If you'd like to receive news of further releases by Clara Benson, you can sign up to my mailing list here.

SMARTURL.IT/CLARABENSON

Or follow me on Facebook.

FACEBOOK.COM/CLARABENSONBOOKS

New to Freddy? Read more about him in the Angela Marchmont mysteries.

CLARABENSON.COM/BOOKS

Made in the USA
Columbia, SC
11 December 2017